"What's going on?"

Rachel's panicked voice shocked Samuel into action. He turned the plane's ignition off and on again, to no avail.

He didn't have much control of the rudder. He tried to push the nose down to regain some elevator authority, but the plane didn't cooperate. *Is this an engine fault or sabotage?* Didn't matter now.

They lost altitude, and the rough surface of the ocean rose to meet them. Out of options, he was committed to landing.

"We're going to hit the water hard. You remember how to deploy your life jacket?"

Rachel gasped. "Yes."

"Remember what I said about emergency landing?"

"Headphones, harness, hatch." The words came out in rapid fire, and he felt grateful they'd gone through the safety procedures so thoroughly.

"That's right. Just do as I say. I'll keep you safe." No choice, he couldn't lose her.

They plummeted toward the ocean. *Too fast.* If the wing hit the water, the plane could spin and capsize.

"Brace for impact!"

Rachel's arms flew to cover her head just as they hit the water.

Megan Short is an Australian author of inspirational romantic suspense novels. She grew up in New Zealand, where her favorite activity was watching bumblebees and daydreaming. A screenwriter by trade, she has writing qualifications from UCLA and has won some screenwriting awards. Megan currently lives in Melbourne and loves learning new skills and meeting new people, many of whom make their way into her stories! She still spends too much time daydreaming and is a recovering chocoholic.

Books by Megan Short

Love Inspired Suspense

Alaskan Police Protector

Visit the Author Profile page at LoveInspired.com.

ALASKAN POLICE PROTECTOR

MEGAN SHORT

Recycling programs for this product may not exist in your area.

ISBN-13: 978-1-335-63884-7

Alaskan Police Protector

Love Inspired
22 Adelaide St. West, 41st Floor
Toronto, Ontario M5H 4E3, Canada
www.LoveInspired.com

Printed in Lithuania

All that the Father giveth me shall come to me;
and him that cometh to me I will in no wise cast out.
—*John* 6:37

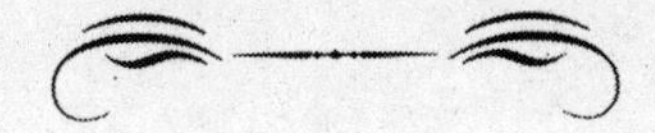

ONE

The distinctive sound of a car leaving the road and hurtling through the railing toward the waters of Eyak Lake echoed through Officer Samuel Miller's cabin. Normally that happened when ice slicked the road and someone took the corner too fast. No ice today. At least not when he'd driven home from his shift in the early hours.

Whoever had plowed through the railing might not have much time.

At the southern flank of Alaska, the sparsely populated town of Cordova lay within the Chugach National Forest, fringed by Orca Inlet. First responders were thin on the ground, so the occupants of the vehicle had little chance of anyone else helping in time.

Samuel pulled on his heavy coat and snow boots, checked the battery on his radio, slung his rifle and a length of bungee rope over his shoulder, and pushed open the back door. His husky, Bruce—one eye brown, one blue—thwacked his wagging tail against Samuel's leg as he bolted past and leaped into the half-foot-deep snow.

The light snowfall brought with it the promise of the long winter ahead, but Bruce could still find a fattened hare to chase.

"Bruce!"

The puppy came to heel with a reluctant snuffle. The obedience had been hard-won, with Samuel having wrestled the seventy-pound bundle of fur into submission until he'd accepted Samuel as the alpha.

They raced through the fragrant yellow cedars toward the road, Bruce panting in anticipation at his heels.

Samuel burst through the trees onto the asphalt and pulled to a halt. A silver minivan hung precariously over the edge of the road. The drop wasn't significant, but a long-enough dip in the icy lake meant hypothermia.

No skid marks. No smell of burnt rubber. What had happened?

He reached for his radio. The volunteer fire department carried the right equipment to do an extraction.

A child screamed, and adrenaline coursed through Samuel's veins. Children had even less of a chance in the icy conditions. He couldn't wait for backup; he had to get them out now.

Samuel clambered over the flattened safety rail and stood within a few feet of the vehicle.

Any movement could dislodge the snow packed under the chassis.

"Help is here, don't move!" His breath puffed out in clouds when he spoke. Thankfully, the stubble protected his face from the frigid air.

Samuel moved as close as he dared to peer into the rear window. The driver sat slumped in the front seat. He couldn't make out much more.

A little girl in a red bonnet continued to yell unintelligibly. *She must be terrified.*

"Hold on, I'll get you out."

Thankfully, the minivan sported a tow ball, which should secure the vehicle until help arrived. He looped the bungee rope around and secured the other end to the base of the railing. The railing creaked when he tightened the knots. Might not hold for long, but it'd buy him some time.

He stepped toward the side door and raised his voice. "Can you unclip your seat belt?"

"Yes." The little girl's voice wobbled.

"Great. Unclip and come toward me, nice and slow." The child's movement rocked the minivan, and Samuel's gut clenched.

She whimpered.

"You're doing great. I'm going to open the door, and then you need to jump into my arms. Can you do that?"

"Okay." A bravado entered her voice and the wobble steadied. Tough kid.

Samuel wrenched open the van door, and the girl tumbled into his arms. Just in time. The movement caused the van to rock forward, and the barrier rasped and moaned.

"Aunt Rachel!" The girl's eyes practically bulged. "You have to save her!"

He lowered her to the ground. If he didn't play this right, she'd panic. He needed her calm so he could determine any injuries to her, or her aunt.

"Hey, it's okay, I'm going to get your aunt out right away. What's your name?"

"Katie."

"Nice to meet you, Katie. I'm Sam, and this is Bruce. You like dogs?"

Katie nodded, reaching to grasp Bruce and hold him for comfort. Her face appeared white and cold. Samuel peeled off his outer jacket and wrapped it around her tiny frame. Although she shook, her pupils returned to a normal size. Hopefully, she'd remain that way.

"Great. How about you and Bruce hang out back here, and I'll go ahead and get your aunt, huh?"

"Will she be okay?"

Samuel squeezed her shoulder. "She'll be fine. I'll get her out in no time at all."

"People die in car wrecks."

Samuel raised his eyebrows. "Sometimes." He considered the situation and remembered her bravado. "You know a lot of things, Katie?"

"Yeah, heaps."

"I like that confidence, kid. Tell me, was your aunt asleep when she drove off the road?"

Katie's face bunched in a frown. "No, we were singing 'Noah's Ark.' Something happened, and then her head hit the steering wheel."

"Okay, thanks, that's real helpful." A head injury, probably concussion.

Samuel turned back to the task at hand. His radio crackled. Backup would be thirty minutes plus; the truck was already attending a job in progress. "Bring the paramedics with you."

He needed to get Aunt Rachel out before the railing gave way. The minivan's side door remained open. The driver's-side door hung over the edge. Should he risk climbing in? Not much choice.

To his right, some large rocks lay in a pile. That'd work. He smashed the rear window with a smaller stone, and it shattered. He dislodged the remaining glass, then heaved a couple of boulders into the back of the van. The ballast might buy him some time. He stole in through the open door and perched on the back seat next to Katie's booster. The van creaked with his weight.

"Rachel?"

The woman in the driver's seat groaned. Good news. Her brunette waves were pulled back in a low ponytail. She wore a crimson snow jacket.

"I'm Officer Samuel Miller. You've been in an

accident. Katie is safe. We need to get you out of here. Do you understand?"

Rachel reached for her seat belt.

"Wait! Stay still." He kept his voice calm but firm. "Rachel, I need you to do exactly as I say. Can you do that for me?"

She made a noise of affirmation.

"Can you move your legs?"

"Yes." Her voice came out weak, but he'd take it.

"I need you to recline your seat all the way back. Can you do that?"

Rachel reached to the side of the seat and pulled a lever. The seat collapsed backward, and the van shuddered. "Katie!" Without warning, she gasped, unclipped the seat belt and scrambled over the seat. Adrenaline.

Before Samuel could grab her, the van tipped forward, flinging her against the dashboard. A horrible crunching sound came from behind to signal the railing sagging under the force.

The vehicle dropped forward a foot. Rachel screamed and scrabbled toward him. He grabbed her and held her tight, preventing her panic from derailing them further.

Only Samuel's knots kept them from plummeting into the icy water. The open door gaped over the edge. They'd have to climb out the back window. He gave himself a mental pat on the back for knocking out that window.

"Aunt Rachel!" Katie's plaintive cry echoed through the van.

"Katie!" Rachel shrieked.

"She's fine. Calm down." The words came out harsher than he'd like.

Rachel's fingers dug into his biceps, her knuckles white. Her breath came in fits and starts. "I can't die like she did." The statement seemed aimed elsewhere, whispered under her breath.

"You're okay. We're gonna climb out nice and easy. Be back on solid ground before you know it." The words had barely left his mouth before the ballast rocks shifted, the railing screeched and the car slipped with a jolt into the lake. His head thumped against the vehicle ceiling, his vision blurred and coldness closed in. He fought to stay conscious.

His fiancée, Amanda, had lost her life because of his mistake. *Don't let Rachel's life end, too.*

Rachel Harding hadn't felt so cold in her entire life. Where was she? Why did her head hurt? She opened her eyes and bile collected in her throat. *I'm going to drown.* Her worst nightmare. Blood rushed in her ears as loud as the water gushing in through the open door to fill her sister's minivan. Her *late* sister. Tears pricked her eyes. Sarah and her husband, Hank—Katie's parents—had died in an eerily similar manner. Six months and five days ago, they'd been driving home when their car ran off the road and into an icy ravine. They never stood a chance of survival. Since then, the thoughts of how much her sister might have suffered, and whether she'd been aware of drowning, had become an intrusive background hum. *Katie.*

The officer had said she was safe, and she vaguely remembered her not being in the van. Rachel wriggled to double-check and realized the police officer who'd tried to rescue her was still there, unmoving. She turned and tried to rouse him. "Hey there, Officer?" She gave him a shake. Nothing. How could she possibly hope to save them both?

The narrow window of opportunity to get them out before the van became submerged was closing. Who knew the lake was so deep? Rachel wasn't much of a swimmer, so she'd never given the lake much thought, aside from its beauty. Today, before she'd set out to take Katie to school, misty clouds had hung low in the sky, and the inky water of the lake lay quiet and mysterious in the foreground. Mt. Eyak loomed behind the mist. The magenta fireweed that festooned the roadsides had withered and died. Rachel missed it. Her visits to Alaska were in the summer, when the fireweed bloomed, resplendent. She was Katie's cool aunt, who whirl-winded into town bearing gifts, sampled Sarah's buttery chocolate chip cookies and then left. *At least Katie's safe.* Thanks to this man.

"Sir?" She shook his shoulders harder. Nothing. "Wake up!"

The plaintive, cartoonlike voice of her six-year-old niece rang out from a distance. "Aunt Rachel? Are you okay?"

Rachel's teeth chattered, and she raised her voice toward the smashed-out back window. "I'm fine, Kitty-cat! Don't worry!" How she hoped that would remain true. She couldn't panic now. Katie had no one else in the world to care for her. Rachel's brother-in-law had been an only child whose parents were long deceased. Her own father had died when Rachel and Sarah were babies. Their mom had passed away unexpectedly the previous fall. Rachel and Katie remained, alone together. No way would Rachel let anything happen to her. To either of them. Katie needed her.

"Come on, wake up!" She gave the man a little slap on his cheek, heat rising in her own—she'd never slapped anyone in her life, let alone an officer of the law. But desperate times… "Please!"

Rachel moved toward the open door, but it had been obstructed by a rock. No choice but to climb up through the broken back window.

She grabbed the back of the seat and attempted to pull herself up and around Katie's large booster. Water-logged and weak from cold, her effort failed. She closed her eyes, trying to think. Maybe if she could fold the seats down, she could climb over them more easily. She reached for the clasp and yanked it. Her numb fingers slid off before she could get a proper grip.

She flexed her fingers, trying to get the feeling back into them, then used both hands to grasp the clip. The seat sprang downward, knocking her back. She landed in the water, soaked up to her armpits. Shaking and shivering, she righted herself and glanced at the officer. The rising water would drag him under if she left him.

"Aunt Rachel! I'm scared!" The familiar wobble in Katie's voice stabbed Rachel in the heart. It brought back memories of the scared little waif who'd raced toward her when she'd landed in Cordova the day after Sarah and Hank had died. She'd finally gotten to a place where the girl could stay in her own room, alone, the whole night through. How much would *this* experience set her back?

"I'm still here, Kitty-cat! Can you be really brave?" Rachel closed her eyes, biting her lip as she waited for the reply.

"Yes."

A whining sound came after her words. Like an animal's. Rachel's heart plummeted. Surely Katie would've said something if a coyote or wolf had approached?

Please, Lord, I need Your help. You know I'm all Katie has. Keep us both safe.

The child still needed help putting on the red

woolen mittens and matching scarf her mom had knitted. Seemed like hours since she'd wound the scarf around Katie's delicate neck and stretched the soft mittens over her fingers this morning. She pressed her tongue against the roof of her mouth to stop the tears, a technique she'd mastered over the past months. The learning curve of being not just a mom but a single mom presented ongoing challenges. Each day she'd learn ways Sarah had done things. Ways in which she fell short in Katie's eyes. The nauseating panic that had gripped her when the brakes failed came back to her. Was that how Sarah had felt when Hank's car had run off the road? A sickening feeling ran through her gut. Her brakes had been fine yesterday, just like Hank and Sarah's. Had someone tampered with them too? And if they had, was Sarah and Hank's accident truly an accident? She'd think more about that eerie similarity later.

"I'm going to go get us help, Officer." Rachel propped her feet on the front passenger seat and locked her fingers around the handrest. Then she launched herself toward the back of the vehicle. The back window was almost within reach. As if in slow motion, her hand flailed in midair, and she missed her target by inches. Her feet slipped, and before she could do anything to stop herself, she fell backward.

Please, Lord, please!

TWO

The freezing depths shocked Samuel back into awareness. Water rushed over him up to his chest. Eyak Lake. Car. Woman. Must've hit his head when the car slid over the edge. The minivan balanced precariously on its front fender, buoyed by the lake. If they slipped farther into the water, it was deep enough to cover the vehicle, and then some.

The woman lay trembling beside him. Now to get them out of the vehicle. The open door wasn't an option. With the latest shift, it had been wedged against a rock. Fortunately, that delayed the water pouring in to submerge them completely. They'd have to climb over the seats and out the back. He frowned. Had the seats been down before? Maybe he'd hit his head harder than he thought. He craned his neck to check the rear window. Unobscured. That'd have to do.

Where's that fire truck?

Rachel's eyes locked on his.

Water had reached his armpits, and he could

barely feel his feet. His sodden clothes weighed him down.

"We're going up."

Before she could respond, he grabbed Rachel near her waist and boosted her through the gap above the seats and toward the rear door. Water poured from her, drenching his face.

"Grab hold of whatever you can."

Her weight lessened. Hopefully, she possessed the strength to hold on. He kicked against the seats and launched his body up toward hers, grabbed her legs, and propelled them up and out the rear window.

The minivan bucked at the movement. Rachel slid back toward the vehicle's interior with an almighty scream. Samuel's stomach plunged. The sound brought back memories so visceral he almost lost focus. *Pull yourself together.*

He braced his legs against the window's ledge and grabbed Rachel's jacket, wrenching her out and up beside him. Her eyes were wide, her face white with terror. "Katie needs me!"

"Hold on!" The voice of fire chief Pete Morrow boomed above his head. *Thank God.* "Catch!" A harness thwacked beside him.

Normally, he'd have a smart retort for his friend, but his head throbbed and his legs were like jelly. He had to preserve his strength. His hands burned with cold, almost too numb to fumble the contraption around Rachel. After three attempts, he secured it; then it took another couple of tries to attach the loop to his belt.

"Ready!" He squeezed Rachel's shoulder. "You're safe now, I got you."

Her body sagged with relief, and she whispered something he couldn't understand. He could question her on that, and everything else, later. He wrapped his arms around her and held her tight so she wouldn't flail around.

The fire crew pulled them up from the water and back onto dry land.

"Thanks." Samuel allowed the firefighter to unclip him, his hands barely usable.

"Knew you'd have things under control." The fire chief's light words didn't match his concerned expression. He patted Samuel on the back and squeezed his shoulder.

No sooner had they unclipped Rachel than she stumbled to her feet and launched herself toward Katie. Bruce blocked her path, his teeth bared. Katie's face held a mixture of alarm and relief. The warning didn't deter Rachel, who looked about ready to shove the dog out of the way.

"Stand down, Bruce," Samuel commanded.

Bruce obeyed and allowed Rachel by. She scooped Katie up in her arms, staggering a little. "Thank God. Oh, Kitty-cat, thank God."

Her raw emotion brought an ache of sympathy to his throat. He swallowed it down and joined them, giving Bruce a scratch between the ears.

His hands thawed in his companion's thick fur. Bruce broke free to lick him, tail wagging.

Rachel turned, and for the first time, he noticed the raised, swollen bump on her forehead. "Thank you for saving us. I'm sorry I flipped out back there." She squeezed Katie's shoulder. "When I slipped down, I thought… I'm all she has." She shivered, and a paramedic approached with a space blanket.

Samuel frowned. "How did this happen?"

Rachel's face paled, and her legs gave way.

"How about we sit down." The paramedic gestured to the prepared the stretcher.

She nodded and accepted the help. Her earnest gaze held Samuel's. "The brakes gave out on the corner. I tried to steer around the bend, but I must've overcorrected. I, um—" Her eyes flicked to Katie, then back to him. She licked her lips. "You're going to think this is an incredible leap, but I believe someone cut the brakes."

Samuel pressed his lips together. *Cut the brakes?* Why did she think that? Before she could explain the statement, they were being ushered away, heading toward the hospital.

Thirty minutes later, Samuel waited in the medical center lobby with Katie and Bruce. The chemical tang of bleach and antiseptic hung in the air. Rachel had suffered a mild concussion, and the doctors wanted to run some tests. Katie and Rachel had ridden in the ambulance. He'd hiked back home with Bruce to change into dry clothes and retrieve his utility vehicle.

"Will she be okay?" Katie's arms were wrapped around Bruce's neck, and his head rested on her lap.

"Sure, she will. The doctors know what they're doing." The words of reassurance didn't stop his thoughts, which swirled around the *what ifs*, the worst-case scenarios. The past. *You can't change the past. Just don't repeat it.* His mind went where he'd forbidden it to go. He and Amanda would be married by now. Maybe they'd be getting ready to welcome a younger brother or sister for Isabel. *Stop it.* He glanced at the clock. Why did the hands seem to move at a glacier's pace in hospital waiting rooms?

Katie pointed to the painting across from them. "That picture's nice. It's like the one in Mommy's room." The mountain range had been painted in hues of purple and white. Interesting choice for a child to admire.

A friendly young nurse appeared. "She'll be out in a minute."

Katie leaped to her feet, dislodging Bruce, who snuffed and stood to attention. "Can't I go see her now?"

The nurse smiled. "Sure. But your dog needs to stay here."

"You go." Samuel inclined his head toward Katie.

The nurse led her toward the rear of the hospital, and a pang in his chest reminded him of another little girl, whose mom hadn't received such a good outcome. Isabel would be almost a teenager now. He should check in on her. It'd been more than a year since he'd called Amanda's parents for an update on their granddaughter.

Soon, Rachel came out in a wheelchair with Katie's hand in hers. She wore dry clothes and held a garbage bag that must have contained the saturated ones. Her chestnut hair hung loose. The family resemblance became apparent now that the color had returned to her face. She stared at Samuel with an expression he couldn't read. He hadn't noticed how blue her eyes were until this moment.

"Can we go to the police station?" Rachel asked.

Samuel had expected to drop her back home. "Are you sure you're feeling up to that?"

"Yes."

Once the nurse had wheeled her to the hospital entrance, Rachel stood, still a little unsteady, and glanced at Samuel with wariness. Did she expect him to say something?

He broke the awkward silence. "I'll drive you. Bruce, come."

When they reached the police station, Rachel deposited Katie in the foyer, where a young officer engaged her in small talk and gave her a candy bar. Samuel took Rachel into an interview room, leaving the door ajar so she could listen for Katie.

"Why do you think someone cut your brakes?" Samuel kept the skepticism from his voice.

"The minivan is barely a year old. My sister..." The woman swallowed like she was holding back a difficult emotion. "My *late* sister bought it when she found out she was expecting twins. They'd be three months old by now." Her eyes glistened, but she blinked back the tears.

Samuel's heart contracted. "I'm sorry for your loss."

"Thanks." She forced a smile. "Anyway, the minivan was new, and I'd just had it serviced last week. The one-year service. I did it one month early, just to be on the safe side. I have to make sure I protect my niece. I'm her only living relative now."

"You're doing a great job. She's a good kid."

A small smile graced her face. "I could do better. Anyway, my point is, the brakes were working just fine. Everything was. I know to you, it must seem like I'm paranoid or grasping, but I really believe someone may want us dead. My sister, Sarah, and her husband, Hank, died in a similar way—their car ran off the road into the lake. Hank was fastidious about servicing the car, too. But maybe the investigation missed something. Maybe it wasn't an accident?"

Whoa. Samuel stretched his hands over his

head. She sounded like a legitimately scared victim adding two and two to get five. He'd been down this road before, and it usually ended in a simple explanation. Sure, he'd have it investigated, but she wouldn't benefit from him feeding her fear. The deaths of Sarah and Hank would've been investigated as a matter of course. If there'd been anything suspicious, they'd know. He made a note on the file to look it up.

"We'll investigate." The *we* was deliberate. Someone else could take the lead on this case. The emotions dragged up today were enough. He couldn't grow closer to this woman and her niece. *What if something happens to her?* He pushed aside his instinct to protect her—which was not easy when her eyes were locked with his. Pools of blue, like Orca Inlet at the height of summer. *What if I hadn't heard the car leave the road?*

Her words broke into his thoughts. "Investigate? We need protection. What if they try again? How am I supposed to protect Katie? If you hadn't come when you did, we'd both be dead." She gulped for air, and her eyes widened with panic.

Not on his watch. "Breathe. Take deep breaths." He reached across the table and held her hands in his. They were soft hands. Not like his calloused, scuffed ones. "In—two, three, four. Out—two, three, four. That's good."

Rachel's breathing slowed. "Sorry."

He pulled back his hands as memories threatened to take over. "It's fine." That came out too harsh. "You've had a tough day. I have a few more questions, then you can go." He asked the standard questions, made some notes. "Where did you have the vehicle serviced?"

Rachel shook her head. "There's only one mechanic in town. Look, I can see you don't believe me. If there had been a problem with the brakes, the mechanic would've found it. If the mechanic made a mistake with the brakes, wouldn't something have happened sooner? It's been a week since he looked at it. They worked just fine the last couple of times I drove Katie to school—exactly the same route, same conditions. Brakes don't just give out without warning."

Samuel's gut churned. Her explanation seemed feasible. But they'd need more than a guess and a hunch to build a case. Investigating the accident would reveal more. Chief Anderson would understand why he couldn't work with a single mom and young girl. He knew about Amanda and Isabel. Samuel's history. *I'll gather a few more details and hand it to the chief to reassign.* "When did you last use the vehicle before the accident?"

"The day before. I picked Katie up from school. They must've done it last night." She shuddered.

Samuel noted that in the file. "All right. The fire department will have the vehicle towed to the shop, and someone will look at it. Until then, the best you can do is go home and get some rest. Wait here a moment, and I'll get an officer to take you home."

Her face fell, and sympathy surged through him.

"If someone tampered with your car, we'll find out, and we'll catch them."

Why did his emotions compare this situation with the other? They were not the same. Rachel wasn't in danger. She bore no resemblance to Amanda, and Katie wasn't reminiscent of Isabel. Amanda had been a larger-than-life teacher, and Isabel had dark features and none of Katie's chutzpah. His engagement to Amanda had been a natural progression out of his caring for them after Jeff's death. *Getting involved now won't bring Amanda back.* It'd only serve to dredge up memories and feelings he'd been carefully burying for the past five years.

Rachel's head pounded despite the aspirin. She stretched her legs toward the open fire, leaned back in the armchair and massaged her temples. What was that cop's problem? She knew her suspicions seemed like a stretch, but she hoped the officer would put aside his doubts to help. After all, he'd saved her life. And Katie's. Memories surged toward her, and she closed her eyes. Never had she been so scared. The thought of how narrowly she'd missed ending up in her own watery grave sent a palpable shiver through her. *Thank you, God, for Officer Miller.*

But then, to dismiss her? What if whoever had cut the brakes returned tonight? A chill ran down her spine as she imagined someone creeping up the driveway last night.

How would she distinguish them from the other unfamiliar sounds of the night? The early-morning snowplow grinding its way along the highway. The wind whipping snow from the evergreens to patter against the windows. Noises foreign to her ears, so used to farm machinery and the rasp of cicadas.

Katie had conked out early, but Rachel wouldn't sleep. Instead, she sat, paralyzed, by the crackling fire. She tried to push the thoughts of today out of her mind, but they circled back around. The crash had been bad enough, but then waking up in the water… *Don't think about it.*

Her legs ached, and bruises covered her stomach and thighs where she'd fallen. Gratitude for Officer Miller filled her heart. How had he managed to pull them both out of danger? She'd not been able to feel her extremities at all for the cold. Strong and brave. The qualities she'd always sought in a man. When she'd been in the headspace for finding a man. Now her priority was Katie. The little girl took up every last scrap of emotional energy she had. Even if she had anything left for a relationship, Officer Miller wasn't her knight in shining armor.

The more she thought about Sarah and Hank's so-called accident, the more certain she became that this was no coincidence. Hank had been a careful driver. Sarah's minivan hadn't been faulty. So who wanted her family dead? The question rolled around in her mind, demanding an answer. Before today, the thought would be inconceivable. Paranoid. Downright laughable. Only, this was happening, and she wasn't laughing. Tears threatened to overwhelm her. No use getting upset if Hank and Sarah's accident was just that—an accident. Even if her gut told her it wasn't.

Caring for Katie had to be her priority. Investigation was the job of the police. And caring for Katie meant paying the bills. Her mind turned to the end-of-month reports she'd neglected for the past two months. Her boss had been understanding with her working remotely—bookkeeping could be done anywhere. But if she didn't get around to finishing this latest batch of journal entries soon, she'd get fired. Then what would become of her and Katie?

A sigh escaped. *Don't feel sorry for yourself.* Her mother's wise words came back at moments like these, and she clutched at them like a lifeline. *Lord, please keep Katie safe from harm. If someone killed Sarah and Hank, please help the police find their killer. I know You have a plan, Lord, but I'm struggling to see it. Please give me hope.*

The next afternoon, Rachel and Katie arrived home much later than usual, relying on a lift from one of the moms at school. They waved goodbye, and Katie bent to pick up a handful of fresh show. She shoved it in her mouth.

"Taste good?" Rachel knew the answer from the exchange they'd repeated every day since first snowfall.

"Cold." Katie grinned, then raced toward the front door.

A gust of icy fresh air from across Eyak Lake hit Rachel in the face and stung her nose. The light had dimmed to black as early evening set in. Rachel still couldn't get used to having darkness by 4:00 p.m. She fumbled her keys and dropped them. Reaching down, she gasped. Footprints led from the front path toward the house. They were large and new—a light dusting of snow had continued until midday. *Someone has been here.* Bile collected in her throat and her stomach curdled.

"Aunt Rachel?" Katie stood in front of her, and her expectant little face suggested Rachel must have missed something.

"Excuse me?" Rachel reminded herself to speak properly. Set an example. No more *Huh*s or *What*s.

"Are we going inside?" Katie scratched her nose where a blond curl tickled against her face.

Sarah's curls. Sarah's hazel eyes. Rachel blinked back the tears that threatened.

"Yes, I just dropped my keys." Rachel bent to pick them up, and Katie scampered back toward the house. *Is someone inside?* "Hold on, Katie, wait for me." She strode after the little girl, trying not to appear worried for Katie's sake. *I locked the doors before we left. It's probably fine.*

Officer Miller's number was saved in her phone. She'd text him when they were inside. No, she'd call him. He could stay on the line while she checked the house.

She dialed, and Officer Miller answered on the second ring. "Rachel? Is everything okay?"

Rachel swallowed. "Hello, Officer. I noticed some footprints around our house." Had she conveyed the urgency of the situation, even as she kept her voice quiet for Katie?

"Is Katie with you?" Having him on the other end of the line brought more comfort than she'd expected.

"Yes, right here. We're outside the front door." Rachel pressed her hand against the rail on the front porch.

"Okay, I understand. Are the locks secure?"

"As far as I can see, yes. The front door, at least."

The officer paused. "Go ahead and check inside."

Katie tugged on her arm, gesturing dramatically that she wanted to know what was going on—the little girl knew the rules of not talking while an adult was on the phone.

Rachel shot her a smile and a wink. No need to scare the girl in her own home. She turned the key in the lock and slowly opened the door.

"Do you hear anything unusual?" Officer Miller's voice sounded serious but steady.

Rachel held up her hand for Katie to stay put, then listened. The clock ticked and the refrigerator buzzed. "Nothing out of the ordinary."

"Great, now how about you go through the house and check the windows and the locks. I'll stay on the line."

Rachel closed the door behind her and bolted it. "Katie, honey, stay with me. I need to check that I didn't leave any windows open."

"Do I get a snack?" The little girl cocked her head to the side.

Not in the mood to hold firm on boundaries, Rachel nodded. "Sure, in a minute."

Officer Miller cleared his throat. "Everything okay?"

"Yes, I'm just going to the back door now." The hallway seemed a lot longer than usual, and she flipped on every light switch she passed. She tried the back door, but it was exactly as she'd left it. "I think we're okay." She hurriedly checked each of the windows, the house now ablaze with light. No places to hide. "We're okay."

Officer Miller let out a short breath. "I'll head over as soon as I can."

An hour later, Katie had eaten her dinner—after the promised snack—and was busy drawing a mountain landscape with her pastels. A knock on the door startled Rachel so badly she jumped.

Katie beat her to the door and flung it open before Rachel could stop her. "Bruce!"

Rachel sagged with relief. She stepped toward Katie and smiled at Officer Miller and his welcome canine.

"Come in, both of you. Thanks for stopping by."

Officer Miller stamped his boots and stepped into the foyer. He made a hand gesture and Bruce followed, bringing with him a wet, doggy smell that filled the room.

"How are you doing? Your head still sore?" His dark eyes shone under the artificial light. He ran his fingers through his ebony hair. Rachel guessed his heritage could have some Mediterranean in it.

"I'm okay." Rachel didn't want to talk about her ailments. "Why don't you come into the kitchen? I can make some coffee. Katie, how about you go get Bruce a dish of water in the laundry? Then it's bedtime."

"Oh, sure! Come on, Bruce." Katie's enthusiasm bit into Rachel's heart.

She waited for Katie's footsteps to recede, then

turned to face him. "Like I said on the phone, someone has been poking around the house. There are footprints in the snow that weren't there this morning."

His expression clouded. "I'll go check in a moment."

Rachel turned to the coffee machine.

Samuel held up his hand. "Don't fix coffee on my account, I won't stay."

His voice seemed neutral, but Rachel sensed the neutrality had been forced. What was on his mind?

"Officer Miller—"

"Samuel. Please, call me Samuel."

"Samuel, have you heard anything about the minivan yet?"

"Not yet, but it's being investigated. I've been assigned to the case."

"That's good news. What about Hank and Sarah's car?"

He blinked. "What about it?"

Rachel scrubbed her hand over her face in frustration. "Doesn't it seem like too much of a coincidence? Sarah and Hank's car runs off the road and..." She couldn't bring herself to say the words. "Then Katie and I have the same thing happen six months later. Now someone's prowling around the house. If Sarah and Hank's accident *wasn't* an accident, then you need to investigate it as a murder."

Katie gasped behind her, and Rachel's stomach dropped. How hadn't she heard Katie approach?

Rachel closed her eyes, drew a deep breath and then turned. "Did you get some water for Bruce?" Did her tone appear bright enough? Her smile felt forced.

Katie's bottom lip quivered.

What had she heard? How much did she understand? *Why am I so bad at this?*

"You want to see a trick?" Samuel's voice interrupted her thoughts. Warm and sonorous. Rachel welcomed whatever distraction he had planned.

Katie didn't speak, but her lip stilled.

"Bruce, come." Samuel patted his thigh and Bruce obliged. He sat to Samuel's left. Samuel held his hand in front of Bruce's face. "Wait."

Bruce's tail thumped the floor.

Samuel stepped to face Bruce and held out his hand. "High five."

Bruce's tail didn't stop as he gave Samuel a high five with his paw. The action brought a smile to Katie's face.

"Good dog. Take a *bow*." Samuel's hand subtly stroked the air downward.

Bruce lowered the front half of his body down but kept his bottom in the air.

Katie's smile broadened, and Rachel smiled, too.

"Good dog! Now, *say please*." Another hand gesture.

Bruce stilled his tail to balance so he could sit up on his haunches with his paws up.

Katie chuckled and clapped her hands.

"Good dog! Sit." Samuel reached into his pocket and pulled out a treat, which Bruce took from his hand. He turned to Katie. "You like that?"

"Yes." Katie's smile didn't falter. "Can he do other tricks?"

"Sure, plenty. But isn't it your bedtime?"

Rachel reached out to squeeze Katie's shoulder. "Sure is."

Once the reluctant but obedient Katie had been tucked in, Rachel returned to the lounge to find Samuel had stoked the fire. Orange flames licked the log he'd added. Bruce lay in a contented half sleep at his feet. As Rachel came closer, his tail flicked lazily.

"Thanks for your help back there."

Samuel stretched his arms over his head. "No problem. Must be tough, doing this alone."

The usual protests and self-deprecations rose to the tip of Rachel's tongue. But this time she grew weary of the pretense. "Yeah, it is."

"Like I said yesterday, if there's something to be found with your van, we'll find it." He stood. "I checked the locks and windows while you were putting Katie to bed. There's no evidence of anyone trying to gain entry. Those footprints you mentioned went around back, then led out into the woods. Do you think someone might have taken a shortcut through your property?"

Rachel's heart sank. He didn't believe her. "Why would they? It's national forest out back."

He nodded. "I'll go check around the boundary before I go, and I'll have a patrol do a drive-by overnight. You have my number, and you can always dial nine-one-one."

"Okay. Thanks." Rachel stepped back to let him pass. But as she followed him to the front door, the power cut out, and they were plunged into darkness.

THREE

She stumbled, and strong hands grabbed her. Rachel gasped and Bruce gave a short, sharp woof.

"It's okay." Samuel's voice calmed her rising panic. "The wind picked up on my way over. It probably caused the outage." He let go of her, and his phone's flashlight clicked on. A yellow beam of light swept the room. "Where's your breaker box?"

Rachel let out the breath she'd been holding. "In the basement. I'll show you." She had no intention of staying by herself, and she could check on Katie on the way. Hopefully, the little girl would be fast asleep.

Samuel followed her toward the back of the house, the phone's flashlight trained on the floor in front of her. The click of Bruce's claws on the hardwood floor next to him highlighted the fact that the wind had died down.

Rachel's legs wobbled, and she prayed whatever the problem, Samuel could fix it. "Watch your step." Katie's LEGO bricks, toys and assorted items of clothing Rachel had meant to pick up littered their path. “Sorry about the mess.”

“It’s fine.”

Bruce sniffed at the clothes, perhaps recognizing Katie’s scent. Rachel smiled at the thought of Katie and Bruce’s budding friendship. Maybe she should buy Katie a puppy of her own. It could double as a guard dog.

Thcy rcached Katie’s bedroom, and Rachel paused. “I’d like to check in on her.”

“Go ahead.” Samuel’s voice came across as if they possessed all the time in the world, which reassured Rachel. If he wasn’t worried, maybe she should lighten up as well.

He waited at the door with Bruce, shining the light on the floor in the middle of the small bedroom. Without Katie’s blue fairy clock, Rachel needed it.

Katie’s soft snuffles filled her heart with love. She reached out to stroke a curly lock from her face. Rachel slept in the spare room, adjacent to Katie’s. She wanted to be close by, but more than that, she couldn’t bring herself to sleep in the master bedroom. That would always be Sarah and Hank’s room. On nights like this, she was glad to have the little girl close by.

“She looks peaceful.”

Samuel’s words pulled Rachel from her reverie, and she stood to face him. She didn’t want to leave Katie alone. He could find the basement on his own, couldn't he?

"After you." Samuel held the phone's flashlight to light her way down the passage.

"No, I'm staying here with Katie. I don't want to leave her alone."

Bruce growled, and Rachel froze.

"Why is he growling?"

Samuel stiffened. "I don't know." He paused and listened, placing his hand on Bruce's head. Bruce's growling continued. "The breaker box still needs checking. You wait here."

Rachel stood in the doorway and peered after Samuel and Bruce. They'd just made it to the top of the basement steps when an explosion of glass filled the air.

"Get down!" Samuel raced back to Katie's room, grabbed Rachel and shoved her to the floor.

"What happened?" Had a tree branch fallen through the window?

Samuel crouched, gun drawn. Bruce stood, alert, a low growl rumbling in his throat. Samuel had turned off his phone's flashlight, but she sensed him turn back toward her. "Someone's shooting at us."

Rachel gasped, fear prickling down her spine. "What?" Where did it come from? How could he keep his voice so calm?

"Aunt Rachel!" Katie's plaintive voice filled the room.

Samuel paused, then let go of her arm. “Stay low.” He kept his hand on her lower back while she crawled to Katie’s bed. His touch reassured Rachel and stopped the panic from bubbling over.

“Kitty-cat, I’m here. It’s okay. Come down here with me.” She pulled the little girl from the bed and into her arms.

“Why are we on the floor?”

“As a precaution. In case something like a tree falls through the window.”

“Oh. Is it storming?”

Samuel’s low voice cut in. “Stay here. I’ll be back.”

Rachel wanted to grab him and insist he stay but could see the sense in him being proactive. To have them all sit and wait for the shooter wasn’t a good idea.

She flinched at the sound of another round of gunfire.

Katie gasped. “What’s happening, Aunt Rachel?”

Lord, what do I tell her?

The back door slammed, and Rachel’s stomach lurched. Had the shooter entered the house? Had Samuel and Bruce gone after him? What if the shooter circled back around through the front door? She’d locked it, hadn’t she? But he could shoot it out.

Rachel cuddled Katie and stroked her head. “Something’s happening outside. Nothing for you to worry about. Samuel and Bruce are taking care of it."

More shots, outside this time. Was Samuel okay? He'd be wearing a bulletproof vest, surely. What about Bruce?

"But, Aunt Rachel—"

"It's late. Why don't you put your head on my leg and try to go back to sleep." Rachel's hands shook so violently that Katie almost slipped from her grasp. She forced her voice to remain as calm as possible. "Wow, I'm so cold I'm shivering. Let's snuggle together for warmth."

"Okay, we can snuggle."

Rachel placed a gentle hand on Katie's back and rubbed in circles. That usually settled her.

The shots had stopped, leaving only the sound of Katie's breathing. What about Samuel? Had it been five minutes? Ten? Rachel had lost track of time, and the power outage meant the clock on Katie's nightstand didn't work. How she wished she were more sensible, like Sarah. Sarah would keep a cool head; she'd know what to do. A pang of grief constricted her throat.

A clatter at the back door set Rachel's teeth on edge. She tensed, ready to defend Katie. Should she tuck the little girl into the closet? No, that would only scare her.

"Rachel?" Samuel's voice echoed down the hallway.

Rachel opened her bone-dry mouth, but no words came. He was alive. The relief struck her dumb.

"I'm turning the power back on now."

Samuel's heavy footsteps reverberated on the basement stairs. Moments later, Katie's clock flicked back on. Rachel pressed the button to stop it flashing, not bothering to set the correct time. The clock's reassuring blue glow lit up the room.

Bruce's claws clacked on the floorboards as he followed Samuel back into Katie's room. Samuel eased the door open.

"It's safe now."

Katie's rhythmic breathing signaled her slumber. "I just have to get her back into bed."

"Let me." With great care, Samuel lifted Katie from Rachel's embrace, slipped her into her bed and tucked her in.

Then Samuel's hand reached for hers, and she took it. Unlike hers, his was steady.

"Are you hurt?" Her voice came out in a rasping whisper she didn't recognize.

"No." He closed the door behind them and walked with a steadying arm around her waist until they reached the front room. "I'm afraid he got away. Must've been a vehicle waiting. I called for backup, but they're caught up on another call. I'll go do a search now." The darkness of his expression suggested there wasn't much chance of finding anything.

Rachel's heart clenched, but she forced her voice to calm. "I'm glad you're okay." Understatement of the year. She shivered. Thanks to the gaping window, the temperature inside and out was comparable. Should she have put another blanket on Katie? The closed bedroom door would trap some heat and the child hadn't seemed cold, but that could change quickly.

Samuel ran his hand through his hair. "I'll get someone out first thing to fix your window, but I'll do my best to board it up now. Do you have any plywood?"

"If there's any, it would be in the shed, I guess. Hank was a bit of a handyman."

"I saw the shed." His eyes rested on the sofa. He grabbed the granny-square throw Sarah had crocheted and wrapped it tightly around Rachel. "I'll be back. Try and stay warm."

He made a hand gesture at Bruce. "Bruce, *guard*." Then he left.

Rachel sank into the chair by the ailing fire. Bruce stood to her right, his ears pricked.

"I guess we should've paid more attention to your growls, huh?"

Bruce huffed as if he agreed.

Once at the shed's door, without warning, the memory of Amanda and Isabel flashed into Samuel's mind. His chest tightened. He'd failed them, and Amanda had paid with her life. The bullets had brought it all back to him. White-hot terror that Rachel would catch a ricochet, just like Amanda had, almost disabled him. Thankfully, his training kicked in. Having Bruce helped, too. But the shooting had cemented the fact there was no choice. He'd have to stay with Rachel. He could see her concerns held merit. It did look like someone was after her, and they meant business. A hard fact. He was off duty, so there was no reason not to stay and help. Not that he didn't want to help. He did. He was just afraid. So afraid of failing again. But could he walk away? Of course not.

The scent of WD-40 and sawdust met Samuel as he swung open the doors to the shed. Rachel wasn't kidding when she mentioned Hank's handyman credentials. Aside from a thin layer of dust, the shed had been kept with immaculate care. Each tool in its own place, everything else stored just so. The workbench cleared and ready for the next project. Extensively well stocked. He probably would've gotten along well with Hank.

He strapped the well-worn work belt around his waist. It held the nails and hammer he'd need to complete the job solo.

The plywood was awkward hoisting into place, but thankfully, the wind hadn't picked up again. He crunched over the icy ground for the last piece, glad of his gloves.

Within a half hour, he'd completed the job. Crude but serviceable. It should keep Rachel and

Katie warm enough. Backup hadn't arrived yet; they were still on that other call. Cordova PD wasn't like his department back in Mayfield. There wasn't an assumption of backup with such a small team.

On cue, his radio crackled, and the chief came online. "I need an update, Miller. I heard shots were fired."

"Yes, sir. No injuries. With the suspect at large, I don't plan to leave the victims alone."

"Agreed. You stay at the house, then bring them in when it's light. Do you need me to send O'Halloran? He's done with the incident at the airport."

"No, sir. I did a quick search of the property. There's nothing obvious. Bruce can help me check for evidence when it's light." Although, aside from the spent casings he'd already collected, he wasn't optimistic of finding much else.

He packed up the tools and returned to the house.

Rachel had relocated from the hearth to the kitchen stove. Sweet smells from a steaming pan of hot chocolate wafted toward him, and his stomach rumbled. He'd missed his dinner, expecting to drop by her house, then head home. Bruce must be hungry, too.

"Thanks for doing that." Rachel filled a large mug for him and added a couple of plump marshmallows. He didn't protest; the sugar would do him good.

"You're welcome."

"I hope you don't mind, I fed Bruce some left-over chicken breasts."

Samuel smiled. Fortunate Bruce. "Thanks." Ideally, the dog wouldn't have eaten on the job, but the puppy had a lot to learn.

She handed him a wrap filled with chicken, lettuce, tomato and some kind of dressing, then poured herself a mug and sat at the table. "Thank you. I'm starving." He released Bruce from his command and joined her, sitting with his back to the wall and taking a bite of the savory food. Bruce flopped at his feet with a sigh.

Rachel blew on her mug, which she clutched with shaky hands.

"I'm going to stick around tonight."

Rachel's shoulders crumpled. "Thanks."

"Do you think you can get some sleep?"

She shrugged. "I can try."

He polished off the food, wishing he had another one, then sipped his hot chocolate. Creamy and not too sweet, just the way he liked it. His eyes rested on her furrowed brow. It'd be a good idea to try to lighten the mood a little, get her mind off things for a bit. "What do you do for work?"

Rachel sipped her hot chocolate. Her eyes gazed into the middle distance. Had she heard him?

"I'm a bookkeeper. Yawn." Her lack of enthusiasm made him chuckle.

"Sounds like it isn't your dream job."

She glanced at him. "It pays the bills and allows me to stay with Katie. What about you? Is policing your dream job?"

The question hit him in the gut. It had been. He swallowed. "I like it well enough." Time to change the subject. "Have you been living in Cordova long? I haven't seen you around." Definitely would've noticed if he had.

"A little over six months, but I don't go out much. Just the school run, grocery shopping and church." Her laugh came out forced. "I should probably make more of an effort."

The woman had lost her family and become a single mom overnight. Socializing was probably the last thing on her mind. "You have anyone back home? A boyfriend? Recent ex-boyfriend?" The question wasn't just for curiosity—the most logical explanation for a stalker could be someone from her past.

Rachel blushed. "No, I dated a little, but no one in particular. I definitely won't be dating anytime soon. Katie takes my full attention."

Samuel swallowed. The implication was clear, and he was glad of it. He did not need the distraction. The evening passed with more small talk and Samuel doing some recon around the property, but whoever had been there seemed to be gone.

For now.

The next morning, Samuel slipped out from his vehicle and walked up the porch steps to tap on the front door. His mouth tasted gummy and stale, and his limbs were stiff from sleeping in the car. He was greeted by a quiet woof. He'd put Bruce in charge for the last hour of the night so he could have a power nap. Thankfully, the hours of training they'd put in were paying off and Bruce had remained in place, just inside the front door.

"Who is it?" a small voice asked.

"It's me, Katie. You can unlock the door."

The latch clicked and he eased open the door to find a grinning Katie, who'd dressed herself, from the looks of her bejeweled, layered outfit.

Bruce licked her cheek, and she giggled. "Bruce, ew!" Her eyes twinkled when they locked with Samuel's. "He licked me again!"

She didn't seem particularly surprised he and Bruce had stayed overnight, and for that, Samuel gave thanks. Rachel could hopefully sleep a little longer. Thoughts of her had plagued him all night. He knew virtually nothing about the woman, yet something about her kept her at the front of his mind.

"My clock went funny," Katie said, her voice breaking into his thoughts.

Samuel wouldn't lie to the child, but he didn't

think a long explanation was appropriate. "The power went out. Maybe the settings got messed up."

"Oh, okay." She frowned. "I didn't like that loud noise. It was like fireworks."

Maybe Rachel sleeping a little longer wasn't going to work out so great for him after all. *Pull yourself together, man. She's a little kid. You have the upper hand here.* He followed her into the kitchen.

"Someone was shooting in the forest." She'd see the window soon enough. How would he explain that? Hopefully, she wouldn't notice the hole in the wall where he'd retrieved the bullet.

"At night? That's dangerous."

"Yeah, I agree." No need to elaborate if she didn't ask.

Her brow furrowed. "What day is it? Do I have to have vitamins today?"

Samuel's shoulders relaxed. "Today is Wednesday, and yes, you need to have your vitamins. You should have them every day. How else are you going to grow up big and strong?" He gave Bruce a scratch behind the ears. "Look at Bruce—he takes his vitamins, and I feel sure he could bench press three of you."

She giggled. "Dogs don't lift weights, silly. May I have eggs?"

The tension returned to Samuel's shoulders. Probably not a great idea to cook breakfast for a child he'd just met. "Maybe your aunt will make you something when she gets up."

Katie shrugged and gave him a sideways glance. "I don't think we should wake her. I can make eggs." She'd give Rachel a run for her money when she became a teen. Katie flung open the refrigerator door, and the bottles gave a dangerous rattle. She yanked out the egg carton. It wasn't his place to tell her to stop, but they'd end up with an eggy mess on the floor if he didn't step in.

"Maybe I should help after all."

A little under an hour later, Katie had been fed scrambled eggs on toast, and Samuel nursed his third cup of bittersweet coffee. Rachel staggered into the kitchen, rubbing her eyes and yawning. The sun caught her disheveled hair, and she smiled at Katie, not yet seeing him. Samuel's heart pounded. He hadn't noticed her natural radiance.

She caught a glimpse of Samuel and startled. "Oh, I forgot for a moment." Just like that, her face drew down, and the light in her eyes died. How he wished he could get that light back again.

"You want some eggs?" He'd been sure to save some warming in the oven, and the mildly sulfuric aroma permeated the kitchen.

Rachel licked her lips. "I should freshen up. Thanks." She glanced at Katie. "You got up early. You've already eaten?"

Katie shrugged. "My clock wasn't working," she said with a hint of sassiness in her tone. "I didn't know it was early." She shrugged again. "I ate my vitamins."

Samuel's mouth twitched. He'd imagined Rachel would've carefully set the fairy clock so Katie would stay in bed until a reasonable hour.

Rachel frowned. "It's okay. You go wash your face. And maybe lose the tiara?" Her gaze locked on Samuel. "Thanks for fixing breakfast. You didn't have to do that."

"It was my pleasure."

Once Katie and Rachel were ready, they all piled into Samuel's vehicle and headed into town. As they approached the site of their recent accident, Rachel clutched the seat until her knuckles whitened. Samuel pretended not to notice.

They planned to drop Katie at school to keep her normal routine.

"Bye, Aunt Rachel." Katie kissed Rachel on the cheek and Rachel reciprocated. She skipped away into the echoing laughs and calls of children in the schoolyard.

"Do you think she'll be safe?" Rachel chewed her lip.

Clouds inundated the sky, and the glare made Samuel squint. "Yes. We wouldn't leave her if I didn't think so. I've alerted the school's resource officer. He knows about last night and your car, so he's going to keep an extra-close eye on her."

"Oh, thank you. That makes me feel so much better."

"My chief wants you back at the station."

"Good, I have questions about my sister's death."

Rachel wanted to curl up in a ball and sob. After a very long day and night, her body threatened to collapse. Samuel had left her at the station while he followed up some leads that had turned out to be nothing useful. No evidence had turned up after a thorough search of her property, and none of the neighbors had seen anything out of the ordinary—much to Rachel's distress, those who'd heard the gunfire hadn't thought it out of the ordinary. At least the police were taking it seriously.

Chief Anderson sat her down with a cup of coffee. The man reminded her of a bulldog: short, squat and jowly. "I remember your sister. She was a nice lady. Helped out a lot at church."

Rachel forced a smile. "I know she loved living here."

"We've pulled up the file on her death, but I'm afraid there's nothing new to report, and there's no way of investigating further. Her car was stripped for parts and crushed some months ago."

Rachel bit her lip as the reality of this fact hit home. *I'll never know what happened.* "Did you investigate at the time?"

The chief nodded. "Nothing suspicious. The roads were slippery, and there were skid marks. Nothing to suggest tampering with the brakes. It looks like an accident."

"Then how do you explain what happened next? How do you explain my brakes being cut? Or someone shooting up the house?" Rachel swallowed down the panic infusing her voice.

"We're still investigating your situation. I have Officers Miller and O'Halloran running down leads, and the forensics on your car should come back soon. We will be thorough." He frowned. "But we need more information from you. Officer Miller said there's no one you can think of who might be doing this, is that correct?"

Rachel wet her lips, rubbing her hands on her pants. "My family was Sarah. My parents are dead, I don't have anyone in my life who would want to harm me. That's why I think Sarah and Hank's death needs further investigation. What if it's not me they're after? What if someone wants Katie dead?" As she said the words, her breathing accelerated.

The chief leaned forward. "What makes you say that?"

"I have no enemies. I have lived an extraordinarily boring life. I've lived in the back end of nowhere my entire life. I'm a bookkeeper! The only suspicious thing that's happened is my sister dying. And every time someone's tried to kill me, Katie's been with me. You can surely understand why I'm beginning to wonder."

Chief Anderson gave a thoughtful nod. "I can see why you might think that. I'll add that to the list." He stood to leave, holding his hand toward the door.

"Thanks." She forced out the word, even as her limbs tingled with the fatigue of the situation. Now she'd have to pick up Katie from school, with a smile on her face, and return home. At least a local handyman had been available to repair the window. Samuel must have pulled some strings. He seemed to be that kind of guy.

"You ready?" Samuel's kind voice cut through her thoughts.

"Yes." She stood and followed him to the car. She didn't want to go home. The thought of staying there overnight sent an involuntary shudder through her. Maybe she should book a room at the bed-and-breakfast close by.

They arrived at Katie's school right before the bell rang. Her scalp prickled when she thought about what she'd told Chief Anderson. Could Katie really be the one in trouble? Who would want to hurt an adorable six-year-old? Parents milled around the parking lot, waiting for their children. Some glanced at the marked police vehicle with interest.

Rachel dragged her body out from the car and trudged toward the gate. A wet nose nuzzled her hand. Bruce. "Hey, boy." She scratched him under the chin.

"I won't let anyone hurt you, or Katie." Samuel joined them.

"What if you don't find them?"

Katie raced toward them, her bright red hat and mittens standing out on the playground. The clouds remained, but the setting sun peeked through a patch of blue sky. Samuel couldn't promise her anything. Not after Sarah's demolished car.

"I'll do my best. Just focus on your niece and let me take care of the rest."

Rachel allowed her eyes to meet his. Their dark brown reflected the dimming sunlight. A slight heaviness entered her stomach. Could he really take care of things? Could she trust him with Katie's life? She didn't have much choice.

Katie flung herself at Rachel and wrapped her arms around her hips. Her chin drilled into Rachel's thigh. Their new routine. Only today, Bruce's snout intervened, levering Katie's arm away from Rachel.

"Hi, Bruce." The giggle in Katie's voice held a rare joy Rachel loved to hear.

Katie rode in the back with Bruce on the way home. She regaled them with stories of her day and ate the rest of her lunch. Hopefully, Bruce would take care of the crumbs for Samuel.

When they arrived home, Samuel and Bruce

climbed down from the car first. "I'll check the house just to be on the safe side."

"Thanks." She and Katie followed Samuel toward the house and waited on the front porch.

Samuel opened the door, and Bruce sniffed, then barked. Samuel reached for his pistol. "What is it, boy?" He held his hand back toward Rachel. "Wait here and stay down."

Rachel's heart jumped, and her adrenaline spiked. Was the assailant inside their house?

"What's happening? Why did Bruce bark?" Katie's voice held confusion rather than fear.

"I don't know, Kitty-cat. Samuel and Bruce will find out. You stay here with me." Had the shooter returned? Surely they'd have been greeted by bullets. Or maybe the shooter had broken in and now lay in wait. What if he'd come back to finish the job? She shuddered, wrapping her arm around the little girl.

"Is it the people who were shooting in the forest last night?" That familiar wobble, the precursor to tears, sounded now.

Rachel's stomach dropped. "What people?"

"Samuel said people were shooting in the forest—that was the noise."

Rachel's hands grew clammy, and she licked her lips. "If there's anyone around, Samuel and Bruce will make sure we're safe."

Rachel's heart remained in her throat when Samuel returned with Bruce.

He gestured for her to enter the house. "Bruce must've smelled something, but there's nothing disturbed that I can see."

They entered the house, and Rachel helped Katie out of her coat, hat, scarf and mittens.

"Can I go play with Bruce?"

"I'm not sure, honey. He might be on duty."

The dog wuffed and whined.

Samuel frowned. "Bruce, relax. There's nothing wrong. Go play." Bruce let out another whine but allowed Katie to run her hand over his fur before she leaped to her feet and retrieved a ball. "Let's play fetch!" The dog trotted after her, still whining intermittently.

"I'm not sure what's up with him. I don't want to ignore his behavior, but…" Samuel shrugged off his jacket. "I'll keep an eye on him."

Rachel glanced after Bruce and Katie, who seemed happy enough playing fetch, then headed for the kitchen. "Do you want to join us for dinner?"

Samuel rolled his neck. "Sure, thanks. Is there anything I can do to help?"

She passed him a potato peeler and pointed to a pile of potatoes, then filled a pot with water. "Katie asked for sausages and mashed potatoes, so I hope you don't mind that. I'll make gravy."

"I'll eat anything." He rolled up his sleeves and picked up a potato.

Rachel turned on the gas stove, but the flow seemed weaker than usual. "That's strange."

"What's strange?"

"The gas isn't working properly. Maybe I need to light a match."

"Hold on, let me check." Samuel placed his hand on her arm. He turned on the hob and frowned. "Maybe there's something I missed. Wait here for a moment. Bruce, come!"

Hearing the command, Bruce immediately dropped the ball and trotted after his master, who headed toward the basement.

"Why isn't Bruce playing?" Katie trudged into the kitchen, coughing a little. "We only just started." She coughed again and rubbed her eyes.

"Are you okay, honey?"

"My throat feels funny." The child blinked rapidly.

Rachel leaned down to look a little closer just as Samuel returned, a grim expression on his face. "We need to get you out of here." He grabbed his jacket, not bothering to put it on.

"What's wrong?" Rachel grabbed Katie's coat and started to help her into it.

"Stop, just bring that with you. There isn't time." Samuel swung the front door open and ushered Rachel and Katie into the cold air. "Looks like someone tampered with the gas line. We need to get out, *now*."

FOUR

The urgency in Samuel's voice cut through her, making her pulse race. "What do you mean?"

"Bruce smelled gas. That's why he was whining. He hasn't been trained for gas detection, but he must've known something was off."

Her mouth fell open, and she hustled toward the car, dragging Katie behind. That explained Katie's scratchy throat and eyes. Rachel hadn't noticed any symptoms herself, but maybe her age made Katie more sensitive.

"Katie, take deep breaths—in and out."

Katie earnestly breathed the fresh, cold air, and Rachel's mind turned to the headlines from last month of that poor man roasted alive from a propane gas leak. What if she'd lit a match? A tingle shot down her spine, and she shook the thought from her head.

Back at the car, Rachel hastily strapped Katie into her seat; then Samuel backed them down the driveway. He parked on the shoulder, a safe distance away from the house.

Rachel caught Samuel's eye. "This wasn't me leaving the gas on, was it?"

"No, it's not that kind of leak." He dialed a number on his phone, and her stomach dropped. Samuel spoke into the mouthpiece. "Hey, I'm at the Lawrence place. Are you in the area?" He listened. "Thanks, Dervla, I appreciate it." He ended the call and turned to Rachel. "I've called the gas company. The tech should be here soon."

Rachel slipped her hands into her pockets.

"Aunt Rachel, Bruce just drooled on me." Katie's long-suffering tone held an edge of humor. *Thank you, Lord, for protecting her.*

Samuel let out a growling sigh and reached for a tissue. He handed it to Katie. "Sorry, he does that sometimes."

"It's okay." Katie swiped at the drool on her sleeve and dropped the tissue on the car floor. Rachel didn't have the energy to correct her. The child was usually pretty good at picking up her trash.

She returned her gaze to Samuel, who reached for his radio.

By the time the gas company's truck rolled up, Samuel had updated his boss, Katie had been furnished with a bottle of water and Rachel had worked hard to keep her anxiety at a manageable level.

A strapping freckled, redheaded woman with a broad smile, parked and walked over to Samuel's vehicle while a young man started taking out tools.

The woman leaned through Samuel's open window. "You're fortunate I was finishing up just down the road. Otherwise you'd be waiting for hours. You've turned off the gas at the tank?"

"Yeah. The front and back door are open, so any residual gas should have dissipated by now." Samuel gestured to Rachel. "Dervla, this is Rachel, the new owner of the house."

"Nice to meet you, Rachel. I knew Hank and Sarah. I'm sorry for your loss."

"Thanks, I appreciate it. And thanks for coming." The words came out automatically, though Rachel really wanted to ask what on earth was going on.

Dervla returned her attention to Samuel. "Evan and I'll go check this out for you. Want to wait here?"

Samuel nodded. "Thanks."

She motioned to Evan, who followed her toward the house.

Rachel ran her hands through her hair. "What are they looking for?"

"A gas leak. I think someone might have cut your gas line, but I didn't see where."

"I need to use the bathroom." Katie's voice sounded strained.

Samuel glanced between Rachel and Katie. "Can you hold it?"

Katie's face crinkled. "Nope."

Samuel drew a deep breath. "Wait here. Bruce, guard." He opened the door and jogged to the house.

"I'm busting!"

"Okay, you can unclip. I'm sure Samuel will be back soon." Rachel climbed out from the car and opened Katie's door.

Bruce turned his head to the side as if to say *I'm not sure about this* and huffed.

"It's okay, Bruce, you can come, too." Katie gave him an affectionate pat on the head.

Samuel jogged back toward them. "Come on, it's safe."

Rachel breathed a little easier, and they followed Katie to the bathroom. Katie shut the door and let out an exaggerated sigh of relief. Rachel smiled at Samuel, who cracked a grin. Rachel relaxed, placing her hand on her chest.

"I'll go check on Dervla and Evan."

Rachel waited by the bathroom for Katie. Bruce followed Samuel. Having them there elicited a mixture of solace and trepidation. She wasn't alone. Yet the reason for their presence… not so great.

Katie emerged from the bathroom.

"Did you wash your hands?" Rachel hadn't heard the water run.

"Oops!" Katie rushed back to wash up, and Samuel returned.

His face had returned to that grim expression Rachel couldn't read. "Someone definitely tampered with your gas line. Dervla and Evan are making repairs, and I have a forensic team on the way to collect evidence. I don't think it's a good idea for you to stay here. Is there a friend you can stay with?"

A tingling feeling swept up the back of her neck and across her face. *Don't blush, don't blush!* The embarrassing truth was, she hadn't made real friends yet. There were a few acquaintances from church and school. None she could ask for that kind of favor, though. Not after six months. But what did she expect? Samuel to guard them around the clock indefinitely? It was too much to ask of any officer.

"Um..."

Samuel's eyes filled with sympathy, which made Rachel's embarrassment grow. He must think she'd failed at life. He probably believed she was not only the kind of person who couldn't protect her niece from harm but also someone who couldn't even rustle up a friend at a time of need.

"Look, I know Katie's teacher."

"Beth?" Maybe that would work. Rachel had run Sunday school classes with her, and she would consider her the closest person to a friend she had in Cordova.

"Yes. I know she has a room available. How about I make a call?" He reached for his phone.

Heat crept to her cheeks and betrayed her. She dipped her head. Maybe he wouldn't notice.

Katie saved her from further scrutiny by opening the bathroom door. Her top was soaked through.

"What happened?"

"I washed my hands."

"And the rest of you, from the looks of things." Samuel chuckled, then walked away to make his call.

Rachel sighed. "Come on, then, Kitty-cat, let's get you into something dry before you catch a cold. I think I'll have to reheat something from the freezer for dinner."

"Aw, not bangers and mash?" Katie's shoulders drooped.

"I'm sorry." How could she make up these compounding disappointments to her niece? *I'm sorry, Sarah, I know you did this so much better than I ever could.*

Samuel's disquiet resurfaced. He'd spent years compressing his feelings into the depths of his soul, and he had no intention of allowing them back. But there was something about Rachel that put him on his guard. The sooner he got them settled in with Beth Ryder, the better.

Thankfully the teacher agreed to host Rachel and Katie for the night. Then the forensics team arrived, and he showed them to the gas line. They promised to update him as soon as they'd analyzed the scene.

Welcoming smells wafted from the kitchen, and his stomach growled. His shift was over, though the unofficial protection detail wouldn't end until Rachel was safe. His nose guided him toward the kitchen. Katie perched at the breakfast bar with a plate of raw vegetables, a carrot stick in hand. Bruce's eyes tracked each bite. Rachel served up a stroganoff of some kind over noodles.

"That smells great."

Rachel startled, almost imperceptibly, and glanced over her shoulder. "I keep leftovers in the freezer for just this kind of emergency. Thank goodness for microwaves and instant noodles."

"Is there anything I can do to help? After dinner we should get going."

"You found somewhere?" The tentative optimism in Rachel's voice set his heart racing again.

Katie's eyes were on him, the carrot dangled tantalizingly close to Bruce's nose.

"Miss Ryder's house."

"Yay!" Katie cheered. The carrot dropped, and Bruce pounced on his prize.

"Bruce!" Samuel barked. The dog quickly crunched the carrot and swallowed. "Naughty dog. You eat last, not first." Samuel shook his head.

"Don't tempt Bruce, Katie," Rachel said. "Dogs find food hard to resist."

Katie frowned. “I didn’t mean to.”

“I know. Just be careful in the future.” Rachel dished up their dinner onto three plates, and Samuel carried them to the kitchen table.

“Where should I sit?”

Katie pointed to a seat at the head of the table. “That’s where daddies sit.”

Samuel glanced at Rachel, who nodded. He didn’t like the idea of taking Hank’s place, even if just for a night. It’d be rude to sit anywhere else, though.

Rachel said grace, and they ate the delicious meal in amicable silence, interrupted by the occasional snuffle from Bruce. The puppy wasn’t one to be ignored.

“You can’t have any, Bruce. You heard what he said.” Did Katie think they couldn’t hear her stage whisper?

Rachel smiled at her plate and continued to chew. How he wished she’d look at him. At the same time, could he afford to connect with her? To his dismay, Amanda’s face flashed through his mind. Rachel wasn’t Amanda, but the feelings she aroused sure were familiar. The situation reminded him of the casual hospitality he’d received after he’d been helping out around the house. Before Amanda had made peace with losing Jeff.

Thankfully, the present dinner was a short-lived affair, and he clicked to Bruce. “We’ll be right back.”

Samuel and Bruce patrolled the perimeter and double-checked the locks and windows before they settled Rachel and Katie into the vehicle. Whoever had the motivation to gas an innocent woman and child was capable of anything, and he'd take no chances. The forensic team had been in and out with no success. The gas line revealed no fingerprints, and no officers had found useful evidence of where the intruder had entered, either. Did they have a key? He should see about getting the locks changed. The night loomed black as pitch, cloud cover obscuring the moon and stars.

He opened the back door for Bruce to join Katie. "You ready to go to Miss Ryder's house?"

Katie yawned. "Yes." Her hand fumbled for Bruce's head. "Will Bruce stay?"

Samuel considered that for a moment. Would it be better to leave Bruce with them? Until he'd been fully trained, it could be a risk. Although, he'd done well last night. "Not tonight." He'd check out the security at Beth's house before he made any more decisions.

Katie's face drooped. "Okay."

After getting everyone into the car, he jumped into the driver's seat and pulled onto the highway. No other vehicles were on the road, and the snow had held off for now. Still, the wet road and freezing temperatures would form ice before long.

Samuel caught Katie's reflection in the rearview mirror. Her eyelids flickered down, heavy with sleep. Bruce's snout rested on the arm of the booster seat.

He glanced at Rachel. "How are you doing?"

Rachel turned her head toward him. "I don't even know anymore."

Samuel smiled back. "You're a good cook, you know." The salty umami aftertaste of the stroganoff lingered pleasantly on his tongue.

She ran her hands through her long hair and fluffed it between her fingers, and its floral scent drifted toward him. "You wouldn't know it from Katie."

"Most kids are fussy eaters, aren't they?"

"Were you?"

Samuel shrugged. "Probably. But in my house, we were expected to clean our plates."

"Did you grow up here?"

"Nope. Kentucky, born and raised."

"East or West?"

"West. Near the Mississippi."

Rachel gasped. "Seriously? I lived on the other side of the river. East Missouri."

Samuel snuck a longer glance—her face lit by the reflection of the headlights, that smile finally back… How could he keep it there? "You probably saw our fireworks on the Fourth of July."

"Ha, you probably saw ours first."

He shrugged. "Maybe."

"Are your parents farmers?"

"Yeah, my brothers have taken over most of that now."

"You didn't want to join them?"

That remained a sore point. When he'd left to join the army right out of school, everyone expected him to return to the farm. His father, uncles, brothers and cousins had all served, then returned to the land. In hindsight, doing that would've avoided a lot of heartache.

He licked his lips. "I'd always wanted join the police."

"You wanted to move to Alaska, too?"

Another sore point. Leaving the Mayfield PD—indeed, the lower forty-eight altogether—broke his mother's heart. According to his dad. The words of that fight rang in his ears to this day. How he wished things had turned out differently. That he'd been able to save Amanda and build a life there. Not that he could tell Rachel any of that. How could she have faith in him if she knew how he'd failed?

He swallowed deeply. "It didn't occur to me until I ended up here."

Rachel laughed. "You know what? That's a great way of describing my feelings on the subject, too."

Somehow those words lightened Samuel's heart, and he couldn't help but smile. No way could he let anything bad happen to this woman. He'd do whatever it took to keep her and Katie safe.

They rounded the bend where Rachel and Katie had left the road. He instinctively took it slower than reasonable, just so she wouldn't feel scared. Still, like this morning, she clutched the base of the seat, and he wished he could reach to reassure her.

"Do you know Beth Ryder very well?" Maybe he could take her mind off that fear.

When it was clear they'd navigated the corner safely, Rachel relaxed. "As a teacher, quite well. As well as our time at Sunday school, I've had many a conversation about Katie's progress since I arrived. She's been kind. Do you know her?"

"She seems fine."

Rachel chuckled. "She *seems* fine? How long have you been here?"

"Two years." Samuel did his best to avoid knowing anyone personally. Some feat in such a small town. He knew everyone's name, whether they were a troublemaker. Just not how they took their coffee.

Coming upon another corner, Samuel slowed again, but a dirt bike swerved into view, blocking the road. The rider was tall and thin, the bike red. He raised a shotgun at them and fired.

Rachel gasped.

Samuel braked and swerved, avoiding the shell. But in that evasive move, he'd driven right to the edge, and there was nowhere to go. He yanked the wheel back, avoiding the drop but taking them right back into the firing zone.

The rider didn't let up. He fired again, and this time the shell smashed through the front headlight of Samuel's vehicle. The vehicle shuddered at the impact, and Samuel gunned the engine. Maybe if he could drive directly at the rider, he'd have to stop firing.

The rider revved the engine and took off. Samuel accelerated after him, but he'd misjudged the corner. The back wheels slid as if he were on a drifting track. Black ice. He gripped the wheel as he fought for control of the vehicle. *This is all I need.*

Rachel's silent scream echoed in her mind as the vehicle slid in slow motion toward the edge of the lake. *We're going to die!* Her muscles twitched, and her breathing stopped as if someone were smothering her. This could *not* be happening. Where had the dirt bike come from? If he'd been following them, they would've seen him before, wouldn't they?

She gripped the edges of the seat, and she turned to Samuel. His eyes were fixed dead ahead, and the terrible, quiet hiss of tires sliding on ice filled the car.

Samuel steered into the slide, then let go of the accelerator and allowed the car to swing in the right direction. The opposite of what Rachel had done. The engine revved, and they were back on the road. Samuel grabbed the radio, and he spoke rapidly. Her vision spotted and his words faded into the background. Dizziness kicked in.

"Rachel? Are you okay?" Samuel's voice seemed far away. "Rachel?"

The car slowed.

She closed her eyes. *Keep it together, Rachel.*

Samuel's hand closed on hers, but she didn't release her fingers from the seat. "Everyone's safe. Take a deep breath."

The kindness in his voice and the warmth of his hand relaxed her body, and oxygen flooded her lungs. She opened her eyes.

"I know how to drive in icy conditions." He gave her hand a squeeze, then returned his hand to the radio. "Thanks, O'Halloran, I'll check in again when I've delivered them. Over and out." He turned to Rachel. "I'm going to retrieve those shell casings, and then we'll get going, okay?"

Rachel licked her lips and nodded, her arms still rigid. She glanced back at Katie, who'd settled back into a deep slumber.

Samuel bagged the casings, then pulled back onto the road and drove at a sedate pace toward town. His eyes flicked in the rearview mirror more than before. Was he worried the dirt bike would come back? Why didn't he say anything?

"That dirt bike came out of nowhere," she said.

Samuel glanced at her, his voice calm. "There's

a BOLO out. Whoever sees him first will grab him."

"We almost died! What if the bullets had ricocheted and hit me? Or Katie?"

He remained silent, and Rachel's mind raced. Did he think she was overreacting? Maybe. She seemed borderline hysterical, even to herself.

She should make normal conversation. Convince him that she wasn't a complete wacko. *Let go of the seat, for starters.* She couldn't.

Rachel swallowed. "How did you learn to drive like that?"

He straightened his shoulders. "I used to do a bit of drifting when I was a kid."

"Drifting?"

"It's a motorsport."

"When you say *kid...*" Rachel would hardly call herself a kid when she first sat behind the wheel of her mom's long-suffering Impala. She'd never been a confident driver, even when the roads were dry and the weather warm.

Samuel shrugged. "When you grow up on a farm, you learn to drive early. Way before you're old enough for a license. Then we—my brothers and I—just experimented. Not much else to do in a small country town if you don't like gridiron and your mom won't let you play video games."

She imagined a young Samuel bumping over cornfields in a jalopy and softened her grip on the seat. "You don't like football?"

"My mother was Italian. As far as she was concerned, the only football is soccer. Any other game's for peasants. Rubbed off on me, I guess."

That explained his darker features. An Italian woman who married a farmer in Western Kentucky. Must be a story there.

"You said *was*. Did she pass away?"

Samuel's fingers stiffened on the steering wheel. "Yes."

"I'm sorry to hear that. It's hard to lose your mom." The pang in her heart at the thought of her mom resurfaced.

He glanced at her. "You've got nothing to feel guilty about."

What a strange thing to say. Should she press him? It wasn't her place. But if she was trusting this man with her and Katie's lives, she had to know more about him. "What do you mean by that?"

"Nothing." His reply was too quick. There was more to this.

They rolled into town, and Rachel glanced at Samuel, whose eyes scoured the streets. He knew what he was doing. He'd proven that when he rescued her from the lake, at the house and just now. If she wanted to keep Katie safe, Rachel had to trust him. *And I need to find out what he's hiding about his past.*

FIVE

The sweet smells of cinnamon and butter greeted Rachel when she stepped through the front door of Beth Ryder's house.

"I've made up a room for you," Beth whispered. The teacher's auburn ringlets seemed newly curled, and she wore a neat ensemble of a dress, blouse and cardigan that reminded Rachel of her own childhood Sunday school teacher. She'd never been to Beth's house before, only meeting up at church or at school.

Samuel carried Katie into the house like she weighed nothing. For *that*, Rachel was grateful. Now over fifty pounds, the little girl became a deadweight when asleep.

"Thank you, Beth. I appreciate this." Samuel stepped past her toward the bedroom Beth indicated, Bruce at his heels. The carpet dampened the sound of his paws, but the smack of his tail against the wall attested to his presence.

Two single beds with matching white metal bedframes and pastel-floral coverlets were set up on either side of a window. A bedside table with a frilly lamp sat between them, complete with a dish of potpourri that filled the room with the scent of roses and lavender. The white broderie anglaise curtains were drawn, but from their size, Rachel guessed a person could climb through if they set their mind to it. She should see that as a good thing—a means of escape—rather than the alternative.

She pulled back the covers, and Samuel laid Katie on the bed. She snuffled and wriggled as she got herself comfortable in the soft sheets, then settled back into a deep sleep. Rachel tucked the covers around her. *Please, Lord, let her sleep well tonight. Send her happy dreams.*

Samuel drew the curtains back and checked the locks. A cloud of mist had formed, and the only light outside came from the streetlamp. She strained for the sound of a dirt bike but heard nothing.

He spoke in a low voice. "It's secure. Come on." He motioned for her to go through the door, then turned to Bruce. "Sit. Guard."

Bruce sat at attention, a grin on his face. Rachel wanted to share his smile, but all she could think about was the way the mist concealed everything. The reassurance of having the husky and his keen sense of smell seemed indispensable. She wished he could stay with them overnight.

She trailed Samuel into the living room, where Beth had set out cups of tea and homemade oatmeal cookies, which explained the baking smells. An oil stove warmed the room.

Samuel pulled on his gloves. "Do you mind if I check around the house?"

Beth smiled. "Sure. Go out the back door, if you like. Through the laundry." She pointed down a passageway through an arched opening.

"Thanks." Samuel walked under the arch. His boots squeaked on the linoleum.

"Come, sit. Have some tea. You must be exhausted. Milk? Sugar?"

"Black is fine, thanks." Rachel perched on the edge of the painted wooden dining chair. She sipped from the bone china teacup. "Thank you so much for letting us stay here. It's such an inconvenience for you."

Beth reached over and squeezed her hand. "Not at all. Happy to help. It sounds like you've had a very difficult time. Katie's certainly been feeling the effects."

Rachel's stomach dropped. Of course this would impact Katie's behavior at school. And she'd been doing so well. Better than before, anyway. Her first year of school should be about fitting into a new environment and making friends, not dealing with this. Her throat constricted as she swallowed her emotions. It wouldn't help anyone for her to shed the tears that had been building. She needed to stay strong, even if she dreaded the answer to what she had to ask.

"What's been happening?"

Beth leaned back in her chair. "Today, Katie told the other children her parents were murdered."

"Oh no." Rachel folded her arms. Another failure. "I'm so sorry about that. It's my fault. She overheard me speaking with Samuel."

Beth's mouth fell open. "It's *true*, then? They were really murdered?"

"We don't know. Maybe. I think so."

Beth rubbed her forehead and shook her head. "I'm really sorry to hear that. I had no idea."

Rachel's heart sank. Maybe she shouldn't have mentioned it. No, Beth had a right to know. "I think I'm in danger." She explained the situation to Beth.

When she finished, to Rachel's surprise, Beth reached to give her hand a squeeze. "It's okay. You'll be safe here. I have excellent security."

"Thanks." Rachel relaxed a little, sipping her tea.

Samuel returned, and Beth gave him a hard stare. "Why didn't you tell me the full situation?"

"Full situation?" Samuel swallowed.

Rachel licked her lips. "I told her everything. Hank and Sarah's murder, the gas line, the motorbike just now. Everything."

Samuel held up his hands. "Look, there's no

evidence to suggest the death of Katie's parents was anything other than an accident. As I said previously, we're investigating Rachel's case with an open mind. I wouldn't bring them to your home if I thought you'd be in danger."

Beth's shoulders relaxed. "Okay. But in the future, please don't keep me in the dark."

Rachel bit her lip, thankful everything was out in the open. She glanced at Samuel, whose face had returned to that grim, unreadable expression. He wouldn't leave them here unless he thought they'd be safe. It seemed unlikely anyone would know their plans, and they hadn't been followed. She'd just committed to trusting him.

Still, the pressure in her chest told her she shouldn't relax completely.

Samuel pulled a sleeping bag from the back and settled in his vehicle for the night. No way he'd leave Rachel and Katie alone, even if they were in a built-up area. Their run-in with the dirt bike played in his mind. He'd called it in earlier, but no one had seen a dirt bike since first snow. Officers had gone back to the scene and gathered what evidence they could, but aside from the shell casings he'd already retrieved, there was little to go on. Most riders had switched to snow bikes already. Didn't help that the dirt bike had no license plate. A police presence would act as a deterrent tonight, especially in the middle of town. At least, that's what he hoped. He cranked the seat back and closed his eyes. Beside him, Bruce curled up on the passenger seat with a huff. Moments later, his breath settled into reassuring, rhythmic snores.

If only Samuel could fall asleep so easily. He wished he could feel as confident as he'd sounded to Beth. But the evidence was mounting against his original skepticism. Whoever had cut the gas line wasn't messing around. He didn't want to alarm either of the women further. Rachel wouldn't get a wink of sleep if she knew he was worried.

Tomorrow he'd go back to Rachel's house and look for evidence. Maybe something had been missed.

Samuel had buzzed the window down a crack to better hear the sounds of the night. A mist had rolled in, and an unnatural quiet mingled with the patchy haze. It reminded him of cold nights on the farm when his family had been happy. While he didn't accept the guilt for his mother's death, his family did. After Amanda had died, he couldn't put on a happy face for his mom as she battled cancer. To his thinking, his staying away had extended her life. What mother wants to see her son suffer? His family hadn't seen it that way. Not being at her bedside every moment of every day had become a cardinal sin. *If only you'd been there, Samuel, my Valentina would still be alive.* The last words his father had spoken to him before slamming the door in his face. He shook his head. The sleepless nights over his mom should remain behind him. He had to focus on the present. Rachel and Katie's safety.

He returned his attention to his surroundings. The fog might obscure a person trying to break into Beth's house. Should he go back inside? The police presence hadn't stopped the assailant firing on Rachel's place; maybe he'd try again. No, this was in town. Shooting at an isolated house surrounded by woods was different from a built-up area where there were few places to hide. He hadn't fibbed about Beth's security, either. By Cordova standards, it was like Fort Knox. She'd invested in security cameras and security screens on her doors, as well as sensor lights. Her yard was well maintained, with nowhere to hide. She'd mentioned escaping danger herself when he'd called earlier, but he'd put it out of his mind. No point wondering. She was safe. Rachel and Katie were safe.

Bottom line, he should stop second-guessing his decision.

What about last time?

Samuel woke up the next morning before dawn to Bruce's huffing, just before there was a knock on the window. He didn't remember falling asleep, but he remembered the dreams. He'd been back in Kentucky with Amanda and Isabel, walking into the gas station before the bullets started flying. Before Amanda had been killed on his watch.

His colleague, Jock O'Halloran, stood outside his vehicle. Bruce knew O'Halloran well—he often had a pocketful of treats. The enthusiastic tail wag said it all.

A layer of ice covered the car, and Samuel was grateful for the sleeping bag. He wriggled out of it and stowed it under the passenger seat. Then he opened the door to let Bruce out for his morning ablutions.

"O'Halloran, what're you doing here?"

The young officer's bright eyes indicated he'd probably had a lot more sleep than Samuel. "Figured you could do with a break. Maybe even a shower. You want me to take over for an hour or so?"

Samuel's heart warmed. He'd notified the chief of his plans to stay with Rachel round the clock, but he hadn't expected his colleagues to chip in. They were busy enough trying to track down the gunman.

"What do you say, boy? You want to go home for some breakfast?" Bruce's tail wagged and he eyed O'Halloran, who took off his glove and jammed his hand into his pocket.

"Here you go, boy." O'Halloran held out a treat.

Bruce gobbled it down, then jumped back into

the utility, bringing with him the smell of dried liver.

"Thanks, O'Halloran. I owe you." Samuel turned on the engine to start the warm air on thawing the ice. Should he go check on Rachel? She'd still be sleeping at this hour—at least, he hoped she would be. He hadn't told her his plan to stay overnight, not sure whether it would reassure her or make her worry more.

O'Halloran shrugged. "It's a slow morning so far. The shell casings are with forensics, but there's a backlog—probably weeks, not days. At this stage, we have no leads on that bike, but I'm optimistic something will turn up soon. Whoever's doing this is a professional, though. There's no usable evidence from the gas line, either." He shrugged again. "He's going to slip up at some point, and we'll get him then. See you back at the station in a couple of hours."

Several hours later, refreshed and fed, Samuel and Bruce picked Rachel up from Beth's house. O'Halloran had reported nothing irregular and left as Samuel arrived.

"Katie get away to school okay?"

Rachel climbed into the front seat, placing her laptop and a flask of coffee on the floor. She reached over to scratch Bruce between the ears, and her floral scent wafted toward him. Dark rings shadowed her eyes. Had she slept at all? "Yes. Thanks for reassuring Beth last night. She was happy to take Katie with her this morning, and Katie loved the novelty."

"She's a good kid."

A small smile. "She is. I wish she didn't have to deal with all this. It's been hard enough to get her into a new routine these past six months without a change in location. Fortunately, she loves Miss Ryder. A sleepover with her is a special treat." She grimaced. "I feel a little bad, though. She'll probably end up telling all her friends, and Beth will be inundated with sleepover requests."

Samuel chuckled. "I'm sure Beth will handle it."

They drove toward the police station.

"Where will we stay tonight?" she asked.

"I figured you'd stay another night with Beth."

Rachel frowned. "Do you think it's safe? I mean, obviously whoever is after us probably didn't know where we stayed last night. But they're going to find out pretty quickly—especially if Katie regales her classmates with the fact."

Samuel considered his words. He didn't want her to worry unnecessarily. "We should get through today and see how things look when I've had time to investigate further. Katie's safe at school. The school resource officer and principal have stepped up security."

She shook her head. "I need to plan. I mean, I'm not a natural planner, but since I've been looking after Katie, it's what I do. If I don't know where Katie's going to be staying tonight, what do I tell her when she asks? Uncertainty isn't good for kids."

"I hear you." He reached over and lightly touched her arm. "Don't worry, we'll make sure there's a plan before you have to pick her up from school." Hopefully, that plan would include Beth's house. If Katie felt comfortable there, it would ease Rachel's burden a little.

He parked in front of the police station and walked around to open Rachel's door.

She gathered her things. "Do you mind if I sit in the waiting room and do some work?"

"There's a spare desk back in the office. Come through with me." He'd rather keep her close.

The station was quiet, with two officers doing the routine security check at thirteen-mile airport, and the dispatcher's radio was silent.

He settled Rachel at a spare desk near his own. "Let me know if you need anything."

"Thanks." She flipped up the lid of her laptop and began her work. The smell of coffee drifted over to him when she opened her flask, and he wished he'd thought to bring some of his own. The break room coffee would have to do.

An inbox full of unfinished paperwork taunted him. He'd have to add to that the report on the shooting and the sabotage of the gas line, too. Samuel ran his hands through his hair. First things first. Typing as efficiently as his skills allowed, he entered Rachel's details into the database. He'd not had a chance to do a background check on Rachel, and he needed to add that to her file. The computer system loaded a lengthy report. Samuel sat up straight. This was much longer than he'd anticipated.

Glad Rachel couldn't see his screen, he scrolled through the report. Rachel's family were no strangers to the legal system. He clicked through to the reports from child services, cross-jurisdictional wrangling, custody disputes.

Samuel glanced over at Rachel. She'd mentioned she'd grown up in Missouri, but was she aware of everything else? He didn't know her very well, but she didn't seem like the type to lie about something like this. Not when she was so keen for him to open an investigation into Sarah's accident.

"Rachel?"

She startled, then turned.

"How much do you know about your father?"

Her shoulders sagged. "Not much. He died when Sarah and I were young."

"That's all?"

Rachel glanced down, her eyes fixed on the desk. "It's hard to talk about."

Was the past coming back to haunt her? He waited for her to continue.

"Mom didn't talk much about Dad," she finally

said. "I know his name is John—that's about it. I mean, it would've been hard for Mom. Probably painful for her to talk about him. Sarah and I were very young. Younger than Katie, even." Rachel ran her hand absently through her hair. "She moved us to Missouri, and I never knew my extended family. Guess I don't know a lot about him because of that. Not knowing became more difficult as I grew older. I longed to have a father like the other kids. But whenever I brought it up with Mom, she'd change the subject. It's something I think about a lot with Katie. Kids need both parents, really—don't they?" She sighed, then sought his gaze. "Sorry, you didn't need all that. Short answer, not much. Why do you ask?"

Samuel swallowed. *She has no idea.* "He's not dead, Rachel. According to his driver's license, he lives in Anchorage."

Rachel's jaw dropped and her face turned gray. "What?"

SIX

Heat rose behind Rachel's eyelids. "That can't be true. He can't be alive. He *can't* be."

Samuel's brow creased with sympathy, and he rubbed his hands on his pants. "I'm sorry, Rachel, but he is."

Sure, *he* believed that, but she couldn't. Mom wouldn't tell a lie like that, would she? She shook her head. Her mom wasn't a liar. "I don't believe it." She folded her arms across her chest.

He looked at her with a thoughtful expression, then reached for his computer screen. Turning it toward her, he pointed to the driver's license photo.

A sudden coldness swept over her. The man in the photo was the spitting image of Sarah. Of Katie. Same hazel eyes, same dusty-blond hair. Only much older. He must be in his sixties. She rolled her chair closer to the screen until she could read the name: Johnathan Maynard Bishop. Bishop, not Harding. But up close, she knew this was her father. "I can't believe it, but you're right. That's my dad."

Samuel placed a hand on her shoulder. She didn't realize how close she'd moved to him until he did that. His breath smelled faintly of spearmint and mingled with the scent of his aftershave. Somehow that reassured her.

She tore her eyes away from the screen and turned to him. "My mom lied." Her lip quivered as the realization sank in. Sarah had never gotten to meet their father before she died. "My whole life, my mom lied. How could she?" She pressed her tongue to the roof of her mouth, and it worked. The tears were restrained, for now.

Samuel gave her shoulder a small squeeze before removing his hand. "It looks like a complicated situation."

Rachel rubbed her face with her hands. "I don't understand. What could be so complicated about it that she'd say he was dead?" A horrible thought struck her. "Is he a criminal?"

"Not that I can see. Like I said, it seems complicated."

"How do you know all this?" Had he been checking up on her?

Samuel grimaced. "It's a lot to take in. Do you really want to know?"

"Yes!"

He sighed, then clicked out of the driver's license image. A weight filled Rachel's chest. She'd had a brief glimpse of the man she should have spent an entire lifetime getting to know, and now his photo was gone, too. Would Samuel give her a copy of it? Would it be weird to ask?

"I'll print out the file, then we can go through it together. There's a lot in it, and it may be hard to make sense of everything at first." The printer clicked and whirred, and she resisted the urge to race over and grab each piece of paper as it appeared.

Samuel stood and walked toward the printer. "The other officers will be back soon. Let's take this into a meeting room. Bruce, come."

Bruce snapped to attention, his ears pricked, and he trotted after Samuel. Rachel followed them past the printer, where Samuel had retrieved the stack of paper, and through to the meeting room.

Two hours later, Rachel leaned back in her chair. Her cramped legs and tense shoulders cried out for relief. After hours of reading, talking and rereading, all she knew with certainty was that sometime after Rachel had turned two, her parents got divorced and her mother changed their surname from *Bishop* to *Harding* and moved them to Missouri. There had been an extended custody dispute, and there were several sealed court files that Samuel couldn't access without a court order. Not nearly enough to paint a true picture of events. Except, as Samuel pointed out, no criminal convictions. All she knew of her father was he used expensive lawyers and lived in a nice area in Anchorage. His birthday fell at the start of April, close to her own.

She stretched her arms behind her and rolled her shoulders. "I need to go see him. I need to know what happened."

Samuel drew a deep breath. "How about I do a little more investigation into him before you do that? You have a more pressing situation here, remember?"

Not likely she'd forget. "I doubt anyone would follow me to Anchorage. I'll be safe enough. Katie can come, too."

Samuel drummed his fingers on the table. "That's not a good idea. You don't know anything about him. Your mom may have had a very good reason to keep him away from you. Don't you think it'd be better to check him out first, before he knows about Katie? There's a lot of custody litigation in there, but your mom still got full physical custody of you and your sister. Probably because it was the right decision at the time." He frowned. "Do you think he could get custody of Katie?"

Rachel pressed her hands to her temples. "I don't think so. I was specified as her guardian in Sarah's and Hank's wills. But you're right, I should check him out first." She met his gaze. "I know it's probably not your job, but...would you find out more about him? Will that take long?"

"I can't use police resources unless it's related

to the case." He glanced at the clock on the wall. "Let's grab some food, then I'll see what I can do."

Research wasn't her finest skill. She needed his help. "Can you apply to get the court documents too? I want to see why Mom got custody."

"I can try." He stood.

"Thanks."

He scratched Bruce behind the ears, and Bruce huffed. "Bruce needs to stretch his legs, too. You want to come for a walk with us?"

"Sure." She followed Samuel to the break room, and a mix of lightness and trepidation filled her. Her father was alive. Maybe she had aunts and uncles. Cousins, even. She and Katie weren't alone anymore.

"Bruce, heel."

The sternness in Samuel's voice reminded her who was in charge. Samuel knew more about her family than she did. The thought sent a tingle of embarrassment up the back of her neck and across her face. How hadn't she known? Why hadn't it come out at her mother's funeral?

Bruce's tail wagged, and he tucked in next to Samuel. The door opened and the faint scent of brine and fish wafted toward them. A horn sounded from the docks.

Samuel put his arm out to stop Rachel, stepped out the door with Bruce, checked the surroundings and then gestured for Rachel to follow. "It's all clear. Let's go. We can swing by the courthouse to apply for those records."

The snow wasn't deep, and Rachel fell into step beside him. A gust of icy wind blew her hair into her face, and she tucked it behind her ears, glad of her coat.

What was her father like? She didn't care—she needed to meet him. What had he done that her mom wouldn't even acknowledge him? Didn't matter—she was an adult now. Nothing he could say or do would harm her like it may have as a child. Or was she being naive?

She appreciated Samuel's silence, as she wasn't in the mood for small talk. Although she'd have had a lot to say to Sarah. Her heart ached. How she wished Sarah could have known. Blinking back the tears, she shook her head.

"You okay?" Samuel's voice brought her back to reality. Would *she* live to meet her father? She had to get her priorities straight. The courthouse loomed.

"I'm okay. Coping. Hoping they have something."

Several hours later, Rachel had found her father only to discover she was too late. The man was dying. Back at the police station, she and Samuel now sat on opposite sides of the meeting room table, hunched over the speakerphone in the middle. The weather outside had darkened to an oppressive dusk. Beth had already ferried

Katie back to her house. After some hesitation, Samuel had allowed Bruce to go with them. Rachel was thankful—Bruce would protect Katie.

"Are you sure the cancer is untreatable? There's really nothing else you can do?" Samuel's pen worked overtime as the nurse gave him detail after detail.

"Sir, this is *palliative* care." The nurse didn't let even a hint of frustration tinge her voice, but a widespread numbness came over Rachel.

How many people must ask these same questions? A brain fog had overcome her, and she wouldn't know where to begin. She was grateful Samuel left nothing unasked.

The nurse continued, "The doctors have tried everything. Unfortunately, pancreatic cancer is difficult to treat unless it's caught early. Mr. Bishop was diagnosed nine months ago, and while he's put up a strong fight, it was already too far advanced to cure. There *really* is nothing else we can do. Mr. Bishop has one or two weeks left to live. I'm sorry you're hearing this over the phone, but when I asked him, Mr. Bishop wanted his daughter to know all the details. He's too weak to talk much."

Rachel's throat constricted, and she pressed her tongue to the roof of her mouth again. She couldn't believe her father was dying. She'd just found him! "May I talk to him?"

"Sure, but as I said, he can barely speak. Do

you have a video phone?" The nurse's voice was gentle.

Samuel leaned forward. "I'll give you my number." He read out his number, and moments later his phone rang. He turned to Rachel. "Are you ready?"

Insides churning, tears threatening, Rachel felt less ready than ever. But this might be her last chance to see her father. "Yes."

He handed her the phone, and the screen filled with the nurse's face. "Rachel, I'm going to hold the phone for your father. His eyes are closed, but he can hear you."

The phone swung toward a man who Rachel barely recognized as her father. His hair had thinned, and his face had paled to almost the color of the pillowcase. She swallowed the lump that had formed in her throat. "Dad, it's me, Rachel."

Samuel's warm hand rested on Rachel's, and he gave it a squeeze, relaxing her a fraction.

"I have so many questions." Rachel's voice cracked.

Her father's lips parted slightly, and he tried to say something. Rachel strained toward the screen, willing him to speak. He let out a whistling sound, and his mouth closed. How she wished he could tell her something, anything, that might shed light on why he hadn't been in her life. Buried feelings of resentment cascaded through her. The years of believing he'd died, each special event at school, every milestone and holiday he'd missed. *Lord, I need Your help.* She stared at her father's face and realized that the man before her was so weak there was only one thing for her to say.

"Dad, I want you to know that I forgive you. Whatever you might have done in the past, I don't hold any of it against you. I'm okay. Your granddaughter, Katie, is okay. We're doing fine." She bit her lip and gave a little sigh. "I'm coming to see you, so if you can hold on a bit longer, I'll be there soon."

She watched her father's face for a reaction. A slight smile crept over his lips, and a tear tracked down his cheek. A weight lifted from her heart.

The nurse's face filled the screen. "I think that's all he can take for today."

Rachel passed the phone to Samuel, trying to sear the memory of her father's faint smile into her memory.

Samuel squeezed her hand again. "Are there visiting hours?"

"There are no restrictions here. Relatives are welcome to come any time at all." The nurse paused. "But don't leave it too long. He hasn't got much time left."

The tears rose, unstoppable. Rachel vaguely heard Samuel say something to the nurse, then hang up. Her head dropped into her hands, and Samuel's hand found her shoulder.

"We'll leave first thing tomorrow. I'll go call Beth." He left the room, and Rachel sobbed.

How can this be happening? Hours ago, she'd learned she had a father. Then Samuel had tracked him down, only to find him in palliative care with pancreatic cancer. A week—maybe two—to live. Would he live long enough to give her answers?

Samuel's heart softened when Katie and Bruce greeted him and Rachel at the front door of Beth's house. Having opened the door first, Beth left her charges to take over the greeting.

He'd been hesitant to leave Bruce alone with Beth and Katie. But he had to hand it to Beth: she knew how to manage kids and animals. And to Bruce's credit, he hadn't disgraced himself or the PD. Katie was decked out in an elaborate costume and smelled of fresh apple and cinnamon. She clutched a wand in one hand and used the other to press a homemade tiara back onto her head.

Bruce's tail worked overtime, and he licked Samuel's hand with unbridled enthusiasm.

"Didn't we just have the fall parade?" The smile in Rachel's voice helped alleviate some of the tension within Samuel. He'd felt helpless today as she went through the roller coaster of emotions surrounding her father. The way she hid her emotions for Katie's benefit continued to impress him. Would she continue to hide them if she knew what else he'd found?

That she was right. The results had come back from the mechanic. Rachel's brakes had been cut almost through—just enough to get her safely on the road until she met a bend. He swallowed down the thought of her in that icy lake. When would he tell her? He shouldn't put it off, but he wanted to spare her the knowledgc just the same.

He also couldn't rule out foul play in Sarah's and Hank's deaths. The circumstantial evidence was mounting, and he could no longer ignore it. Based on the professional level of attacks on Rachel and the surrounding circumstances, a carefully concealed sabotage to Hank's car was probable.

The bigger questions surrounded how to handle Rachel's safety. The person was after Rachel for sure. However, based on the evidence, he might not intend to harm Katie. If he did, he could've staged Sarah and Hank's accident at a time Katie was in the car, too. If Samuel was right and Rachel was the true target, wouldn't it be safer for Katie to stay with Beth until the perpetrator was incarcerated?

Katie bounced up and down, her fairy wings flapping. "We're helping Miss Ryder with the costumes for the Thanksgiving parade! Bruce is a superhero because he's brave." That explained the handkerchief clipped to Bruce's collar. What a relief, to know that Bruce's first day without him had been successful. Seemed Bruce's good nature extended to Katie's antics, and his protective instinct wasn't limited to training drills. This was good experience for the puppy if he was going to work as a multipurpose dog.

Beth called from the other room, "Come in and shut the front door. I can feel the breath of the snow queen from here!"

Katie giggle with delight. "The snow queen will turn your heart to *ice*, Aunt Rachel!"

"Well, we don't want that, now, do we?" Rachel winked at Samuel, then held his gaze.

The intimacy kicked his heart rate up a notch, and he turned to break eye contact. *That's too intense.* He closed the door and fumbled the lock, forcing his heart to calm down. Then he followed the procession into the kitchen.

Colored craft and crepe paper, glue, scissors, markers, glitter, Popsicle sticks, paint, string, tape and other assorted materials bedecked the newspaper-covered table, including several half-completed projects, mostly turkey themed.

Katie thrust her hands over one of them with a stricken expression. "Don't look, it's not finished!"

Rachel covered her eyes and turned away. "I didn't see anything, I promise."

"Phew!"

Beth caught Samuel's eye with a smile. "How about you-all go into the living room, and we can clean up to get ready for dinner."

Samuel wanted to speak with Beth alone, but it didn't look like that would happen until the festivities were cleared away. Instead, he followed Rachel.

"Thanks for leaving Bruce with Katie." Rachel sank into a plush armchair near the oil heater.

"I think he's turning out to be a natural at protection."

Rachel massaged her temples with her fingertips. "I'm just grateful to see her happy. If Bruce can stay here with her, maybe she'll be safer than she'd be with us in Anchorage." She opened her eyes. "Do you think he could stay?"

Samuel nodded. Beth had proved she could handle Bruce, and it would only be for part of the day. "I doubt the hospital will let him in, anyway. O'Halloran can take care of him while they're at school."

"Couldn't he go to school with them?"

"No. Bruce spent some time at the school as a younger puppy to see if he would be suitable as an emotional support dog. He failed miserably."

Rachel shrugged. "He seems like pretty good emotional support to me."

"Support dogs need to be predictable and calm at all times. You may have noticed that Bruce is a little too excitable to be described as that."

She smiled. "True."

"Anyway, while the experience acclimated him to kids, he's a working dog. He should be at the PD. I'll have to check if Beth's okay with the plan."

"What plan?" Beth's voice preceded her entrance, and she poked her head through the doorway.

Samuel stood. "We need to head to Anchorage for the day, and I can't take Bruce. Are you okay with keeping him here until O'Halloran picks him up tomorrow?"

Katie pushed past Beth, with a rustle of tulle and sequins, and skipped toward Rachel. "You can come in now!"

Rachel quickly forced a smile. "I'm glad to hear that."

Beth glanced between them. "I think we should discuss the logistics, but the answer's yes."

Early the next morning, Samuel climbed into the seat of the floatplane and helped Rachel to secure her seat belt and orientate her headphones.

He'd insisted she wear the manually inflatable life jacket that he'd brought from home—an old habit his dad had taught him. *Always bring a life jacket you know you can trust.* Once buckled in, she adjusted it several times before she seemed comfortable, then settled with a sigh.

He'd called the flight company last night to book a floatplane and had given the attendant their flight plan, including his and Rachel's details. They now sat in the only one available, a 1975 Cessna A185F. He'd flown similar planes before, and with the weather in their favor—so far—he figured they'd reach Anchorage by ten in the morning. It'd give them some space from Cordova and whoever was after Rachel. He'd decided to tell her about the brakes after she'd seen her father. It wouldn't serve a purpose to tell her before then. It would only cause her more anxiety and fear.

"Can you hear me?" Her words came through the headphones clearly. He enjoyed the sound of her voice so close by.

"Loud and clear. You ready?"

"Yes, I'm ready." Rachel seemed more relaxed this morning. Katie had gone to bed exhausted and happy. They'd stayed up late with Beth, explaining the situation with Rachel's father. Beth had been sympathetic and kind, willing to care for Katie as long as needed. Maybe that explained why Rachel had slept better last night.

Samuel had not. Apart from the discomfort of sleeping in his car, he worried over their not having contact with the perpetrator that day. The person's pattern was one of escalation, so what was he waiting for? Would it come in the early hours? He'd hoped him being outside would act as a deterrent. It'd also be riskier to open fire in town than out near the forest, with most citizens armed and ready to shoot back. Still, he'd spent the night on edge.

Despite some patchy fog, Orca Inlet presented good conditions for takeoff. That could change quickly, especially with Alaska's unpredictable weather. Hopefully, when they returned, landing conditions would be as good as this. Still, Samuel always prepared for the worst. He'd checked to make sure they had a life raft in the seat behind them, and he'd packed his own emergency beacon just in case.

Samuel went through the *before takeoff* checklist, then taxied past a raft of sea otters into the middle of the channel.

"They are so cute!" Rachel leaned over to get a closer look. "I love how they have their own special rocks."

Samuel's heart warmed at her enthusiasm. The engine buzzed as he engaged full throttle, and the plane took off into the wind. They climbed and turned toward Anchorage. The plane leveled out and they flew over Hawkins Island, its rounded tops now brushed with snow.

He briefly turned toward her. "All good?"

"Oh yes! Isn't the view amazing! Are those black-tailed deer?" Rachel's voice seemed natural.

"Yeah."

She rubbed her legs. "It's cold, though."

The plane was unheated, so *cold* was an understatement. Even so, a warmth rose within him. "You like flying?"

"Beats the ferry, that's for sure. When did you learn to fly? Don't tell me... On the farm?"

Samuel chuckled. "Yeah, I did my fair share of crop-dusting. But floatplanes are new. I learned when I arrived. Gives me the freedom to come and go without relying on the ferry or airline's timetables." He checked the landing conditions as more words of his father's rang in his ears: *Make sure you have a plan for landing at all times.* Could it be the impending death of Rachel's father that had his own in his head? Either way, it reassured him, even if the old man wouldn't take his calls. The water was a little choppy, but nothing too dramatic.

"I can understand that. Sometimes I wish I could fly off into the sunset." A wistfulness entered her tone. "But the feeling passes as soon as Katie smiles at me." Rachel leaned forward in her seat. "Hey, look at those clouds coming in over the glacier."

He'd seen them, and the wind that promised to kick up the waves over Prince William Sound. "We should be past Whittier before they come any closer."

"Okay, that's good." She settled back into her seat. "I've never seen the Colombia Glacier from the sky, just from the ferry. What a different perspective!"

He pointed to his left. "And that's Montague Island."

They continued toward the middle of Prince William Sound.

He reached for the radio to confirm their position, but the radio crackled, then failed. He turned it off and on again, but nothing happened. He'd checked the plane thoroughly before takeoff, making sure everything was in working order, so what was the deal with this?

"What's wrong?" Rachel's voice had lost its contentedness. He couldn't allow the worry to overtake things now. She needed to be able to meet with her father without fear hanging over her.

"The radio has a fault. It's okay, we can land without it."

Rachel's brow creased. "Are you sure?"

"Yeah, nothing to worry about. We'll touch down in Anchorage before you know it."

The engine revved, then lost power. The plane started gliding. A surge of adrenaline prickled through his limbs. This could not be happening. There'd been absolutely nothing off in his precheck.

"Samuel? What's going on?"

Rachel's panicked voice shocked him into action. He turned the ignition off and on again, to no avail. He checked the controls. The voltage seemed good, but there was no fuel pressure. Maybe a cracked fuel rail?

He didn't have much control of the rudder. He tried to push the nose down to regain some elevator authority, but the plane didn't cooperate. It didn't make sense. The plane wouldn't behave like this for just a cracked fuel rail. *Is this an engine fault or sabotage?* Didn't matter now.

They lost altitude, and the rough surface of the ocean rose to meet them. Out of options, he was committed to landing.

"We're going to hit the water hard. You remember how to deploy your life jacket?"

Rachel gasped. "Yes." She fumbled for the tags, patting them.

"Remember what I said about emergency landing?"

"'Headphones, harness, hatch.'" The words came out rapid-fire, and he felt grateful they'd gone through the safety procedures so thoroughly. Getting tangled in a headphone cable on the way out could prove disastrous.

"Good girl, that's right. Just do as I say. I'll keep you safe." No choice—he couldn't lose her.

They plummeted toward the ocean. *Too fast.* If the wing hit the water, the plane could spin and capsize. Samuel used what little control he had to keep the plane steady and hoped it would be enough.

"Brace for impact!"

Rachel's arms flew up to cover her head just as they hit the water.

The left float of the plane pierced the surface first and submerged. The floatplane juddered, tossing them to and fro, and Rachel screamed. Samuel turned the plane toward the drowned float. Would the reduced speed and the turn lessen the damage? The wing tipped into the water, and the plane spun 180 degrees. Their heads jerked from side to side, and Rachel grabbed the headphones, locking her forearms against her side. As they came to a stop, waves buffeted the floatplane and it tilted to the left. They were taking on water!

Rachel's face turned ashen, eyes wide, and she still gripped her headset. "What now?"

Samuel unclipped his harness so he could reach behind for the life raft. He grabbed the emergency beacon he'd packed and turned it on. Rachel's hand shook uncontrollably. When he grabbed it to slip the strap around her wrist, her skin felt like ice.

"Headset, harness, hatch. Then jump out and inflate your life jacket. Now!"

He didn't wait for a reply, yanking off his own headset. He'd have to climb out Rachel's hatch, as his was already underwater. They had a minute or two before remaining in the plane became dangerous.

Fortunately, Rachel had climbed out of the

plane and jumped into the water by the time he'd reached the hatch. He pushed the life raft after her, fastened it to the doorframe and then threw it far as he could from the plane, a few feet from Rachel. She'd deployed her life jacket with no issues. When the cable pulled taut, he tugged the lanyard to deploy it. As he did so, a large wave crashed into the plane.

The cabin tilted, and he fell inside, engulfed by salt water. His back hit the stick, and he flailed behind to grab it. The cabin flooded, the icy water climbing past his waist and up to his armpits, then lapping his neck. Crushing cold sliced through his outwear, shocking the air out of his lungs. He forced a last gasp of oxygen before he went under. One of the plane's floats had stayed buoyant. If it filled, he'd be in trouble. He pushed through the water toward the hatch. It had snapped shut. *Please open.*

He pressed the hatch with sustained force, but nothing happened. His lungs burned, and his limbs seized with the cold. Should he keep trying or go to the other one? It'd opened before. It had to open again. He gave it a shove, but it remained stuck. *I'll black out if I don't get free soon!* Then what would happen to Rachel?

SEVEN

Rachel's heart hammered when she leaped into the water. The plane's unexpected descent had left her reeling, and the adrenaline continued to surge through her. She'd heard of light planes going down in Alaska but never expected it to happen to her. Car accidents were much more likely. Her first thought had been sabotage, but she'd quickly dismissed the idea. Surely it'd be too difficult to make a plane come down in the middle of Prince William Sound. More likely, it had been an accident, a plane fault of some kind. No point wondering about hypotheticals. Still, the lingering fear that someone might have caused the crash ran through the back of her mind. What if they came to make sure they were dead? She shuddered.

Unlikely. Samuel managing to get them down without crash-landing had been extraordinary. They *should* be dead. Her mind turned to the other possibilities, but she pushed them away. Samuel knew what he was doing. Thanks to him, they'd survived so far; no use dwelling on *what ifs*.

The freezing temperature shocked the air out of her lungs, and she began to hyperventilate. Her breathing grew very fast and deep, uncontrollable. What was happening to her body? The frigid water soaked through her clothes and weighed down her shoes. Struggling to keep her head away from the waves, fearful she'd suck in seawater, she turned her face toward the sky. The clouds she'd seen earlier rolled in fast, and the sky darkened. Would rescuers be able to see them? Had she been saved from the lake only to drown in the ocean? Fear gripped her stomach like a vise. *No, don't panic. Katie needs you.* She gritted her teeth. *Focus!*

Waves pushed her away from the floatplane, and she turned to look for Samuel. She startled when a yellow-and-orange life raft self-inflated before her. Grateful that Samuel was well prepared, she kicked toward it, floating on her side to keep the water from flowing over her face. She turned to check her surroundings. The raft obscured her view of everything else, including the plane. Was Samuel still inside? She should get herself to safety first so that he didn't have to worry about her. Her body ached from the cold, and her arms and legs felt heavy. Blood must be making its way to her body, protecting her internal organs. She'd obsessively searched for such facts after Sarah and Hank's accident. As if knowing the full details would help her come to terms with what they'd suffered. It hadn't. But she knew that ten to thirty minutes was the window for survival. Not long. She had to move.

Spitting icy salt water from her mouth, she reached the side of the life raft and grabbed one of the handles. The emergency beacon clanged against the side of the raft. Would help come soon? Her teeth chattered. She attempted to pull herself up into the raft, but her frozen hands slid off the side. Water splashed on her face, shocking her. *I'm too weak.*

She'd never meet her father. Katie would lose her as well. At least she had Beth. Tears pricked her eyes. Maybe Beth would be a better guardian than her. *Stop feeling sorry for yourself!* Samuel might be in the raft. He'd pull her in. But why hadn't he looked for her?

"Samuel?" Her voice came out as a weak gasp. No way he'd hear her. She kicked as hard as she could and, with her best effort, pulled her body up and into the raft. The cover came up and stopped her from seeing much. But Samuel wasn't in the raft. Her breathing slowly returned to normal.

"Samuel!"

The raft bobbed violently on the waves, tumbling her around, and fingers of dread crawled up her spine. How sturdy was the raft? Her mind grew foggy. She rubbed her hands along her arms in a futile attempt to warm up. Where was Samuel? She peered around the cover and gasped. The floatplane had inverted! Surely he wasn't still inside. *Please, Lord, no!*

She swept her gaze around the plane, searching for any sign of Samuel. He hadn't been behind her, wasn't in the raft. He must be inside the plane.

"Samuel!" Tears warmed her frozen cheeks, and she wiped them away, the sting of warmth on her fingertips reminding her of the frozen water. If she swam back to him, it was doubtful she'd survive. Could she get to him using the raft? She searched the raft for a rope or something else she might be able to use. A lanyard had been fastened to the raft with a ring on the end. Not long enough to secure her and give her the length she'd need to reach the plane. She searched further, found a water bailer. That'd be about as effective as her hands. A numb despair filled her. How long had it been? She wouldn't reach Samuel in time. Sorting half-heartedly through the remaining provisions, she found a flashlight.

A flashlight! Yes, it *was* waterproof. She checked to ensure it worked, pulled the strap around her other wrist and plunged her hand into the water, ignoring the pain of the coldness. She turned it on and off, on and off. If he'd become disoriented, maybe Samuel would head for the light.

"Please, Lord, save Samuel. Please don't let him die out here alone."

Samuel's stomach clenched as he tried the hatch again. Was it properly jammed? No time to find out. He pulled himself toward the other hatch and yanked the handle. It slowly swung through the water. He was free!

Samuel swam through the hatch and away from the plane. He kicked toward the surface, but his limbs were sluggish in the icy water, like he was flailing in molasses. Fear gripped him. Where was the surface? *Bubbles rise to the surface.* The water before him had darkened.

He let out some of his precious oxygen. Zero visibility. His chest ached, and not only from the lack of air. *I've left so much undone.* The melancholic thought caught him by surprise, and he let more oxygen escape until his lungs were almost empty.

A light clicked on, then off. On, then off. The light illuminated the bubbles. He knew where he had to go. Kicking hard, impaired by his heavy clothes and freezing body, he rose to the surface. Gasping for air, he yanked on the straps of his life jacket to inflate it.

"Samuel!" Rachel's voice welcomed him.

He couldn't speak, just let the waves lap over

him. A small ring attached to a hauling line thwacked him right in the face, snapping him out of his daze.

"Sorry! Grab hold!"

Samuel grasped the ring as best he could and allowed Rachel to haul him toward the life raft. He regained control of his faculties in the last few feet and kicked toward her.

"Here, take my hand."

He ignored the offered hand, knowing she couldn't possibly haul him into the raft, and with the last of his strength, he pulled himself in beside her.

She grabbed him in an unexpected embrace, her entire body shivering. "Thank God you're okay. I thought you'd…" She squeezed him, then let go. He wished she'd held him a little longer. His mind swept back to his dying thought, of all he'd left undone. Now Rachel filled his mind. *I wouldn't have gotten to kiss her if I died.* Where did that thought come from? Rachel was a victim, not someone with whom he could have any romantic involvement. Even if he could, would he want to? Could he risk the pain he'd experienced when Amanda died? Or the destruction that pain had caused his family?

He allowed his eyes to rest on Rachel's face. Even with her hair messed and straggly, her lips chapped, and her face mottled with cold, she caused a flicker in his heart. Could he act on that? Nope. He had to accept that his life would always be lonely. A life of penance.

Besides, if the plane had been sabotaged, they remained in imminent danger. He should focus on protecting Rachel, not his confusing feelings.

"Do you have the emergency beacon?"

"Yeah, it's here." She held up her wrist. The aerial would work best upright, but it was impossible to achieve with the raft pitching and heaving on the waves.

"That's good. Help should already be on the way." Was that true? Sometimes it took several hours for a satellite to pass by and see a GPS beacon. His body shivered, and his teeth chattered uncontrollably. He wrapped his arms around himself and rubbed his hands up and down his arms. Not much use, but maybe it'd guard his fingers from frostbite.

Rachel zipped up the cover with shaking hands. "There's a wall of rain closing in. We don't want the raft to flood." She rummaged around in a pack that must've been in the life raft. She pulled out two bright orange thermal protective aids and unfurled them with shaking hands.

"Can you climb into this?"

Samuel uncurled his fingers from around his arms with some effort and leaned toward her. No frostbite…so far. She laid one of them out, and he wrestled his legs into the opening. The aluminized polyethylene material rustled and fussed, but he got his arms in, and Rachel fastened it for him. *I should be the one helping her.*

"All good?"

"Yeah, thanks." The chattering of his teeth slowed, though the shivering remained.

Her grin broadened, and she chuckled.

"What?"

"I apologize, it's just…" She chuckled again. "You look like you're wearing a lobster costume. But I shouldn't laugh, because I'm next."

Rachel slipped into her own TPA with a lot more gracefulness, but as she kneeled to fasten it, a wave hit the raft at the wrong moment and sent her off-kilter. She fell onto Samuel, and he caught her, his arms regaining their feeling when he wrapped them around her.

"I'm sorry."

"Not your fault." Against every instinct to embrace her until help arrived, he set her upright, easing her to sit next to him and readjusting both their TPAs. She was right about the lobster comment. Together they must look ridiculous. Hopefully, someone would find them soon enough to appreciate the joke.

A sudden downpour drowned out her next words. Thank goodness she'd had the foresight to close the roof over them. The raft rocked in the waves, and the salty, dank smell reminded him of the boatsheds in wet weather.

How long had it been since he'd set off the

emergency beacon? In weather like this, even if they'd seen the signal, the coast guard would find it hard to attempt a rescue. He leaned over and talked directly into her ear.

"Are you injured?"

She shook her head, then turned to speak into his ear. "I'm fine. Just cold. How about you?" Her breath warmed him, and his ear stung as the feeling returned.

"All in a day's work."

She laughed, as he'd hoped she would, most of the sound smothered by the rain. The expression on her face was enough to keep him going. They could be on the water for some time. They should probably collect fresh water while it rained.

The feeling had returned to his extremities, but it didn't seem to have the retained coldness he'd expect from frostbite. They'd have to get checked out—if they survived. Time for him to look after her. "Is there a bottle or a bucket in here?" He raised his voice to be heard.

She shrugged and pointed to a bag of supplies. He scooched over to look. They'd been fortunate with the TPAs. Everything else preserved the raft rather than the occupants. The bailer would help collect some rain to hydrate them now, but it wouldn't help later if this dragged on.

He turned back and noticed Rachel's head bowed, her eyes closed and her hands clasped in front of her in prayer. Samuel's gut clenched. He'd allowed his prayer life to atrophy after Amanda. She'd be ashamed of him if she knew. Maybe now was a good time to begin again. *Lord, I promise, I want to live, and if You see fit to make that happen, I'll do better. And if that's not to be, then... forgive me for all the things I've left unsaid and undone. I'm sorry. But most of all, please take care of Katie.*

He unzipped the cover enough to stick his hand out with the bailer. The chill returned when the heavy rain ran down his arm, but it filled the bailer quickly. He brought it back, carefully balancing it with the waves. He took a sip. Sweet water rinsed the brackish taste from his mouth. He didn't want to interrupt Rachel's prayer, so he drank his fill first, then gathered some more. Once he'd zipped the cover, he brought the bailer to Rachel.

"Thanks." She drank like she needed it, finishing it all.

"More?"

She shook her head. He filled it again for later and set it aside, careful to make sure it wouldn't tip over.

The rain eased to a steady thrum.

"What happened with the plane?" Rachel raised her voice to be heard, but it failed to mask the fear within the question.

Should he share his suspicions? No point trying to protect her fear levels now. *We might die here*. Did he want her last memories to be filled with thoughts of the threats to her life? *They probably are already.*

"Samuel?"

"I don't know." The truth.

"You think it was sabotage?" Her head bowed. "I mean, unless you think the jury's still out on what happened to our van."

He swallowed. "No, the brakes were cut."

Rachel gave him an *I-told-you-so* look. "So, likely the plane *was* tampered with."

"No way we can conflate the two. We need to get the plane examined to work out what went wrong."

"You know about planes. What's your theory?" Her earnest expression triggered that protective instinct within him. She was the victim, not a cop. If these were her final moments, it wouldn't help her to spend them with thoughts like that.

"Let's concentrate on surviving. We can investigate the plane when we're safe."

Her shoulders slumped. "You're right. We have to survive first."

They lapsed into silence, and the rain petered out to a drizzle, then a light mist. Samuel unzipped the cover to see where they were. The fresh smell of rain and brine blended with the surrounding fog. Day headed toward dusk. They'd been out here for hours. Would they be here all night? The temperature would drop even further.

"Where are we?" she asked.

Samuel zipped the cover back into place to preserve their warmth. His clothes clung to him and chafed uncomfortably. His skin was damp and waterlogged, but at least he could feel his extremities.

"Floating somewhere in Prince William Sound." He reached for her wrist, her hand barely warmer than before. "Here, I'll float this on the water. It's calmer now, might give a better signal." He attached the emergency beacon to a lanyard and floated it outside the raft. The aerial upright, the light flashing. No one would see them in this fog; they'd be reliant on the GPS. Would they even attempt a rescue? Probably too risky. He sighed.

"Are you okay?"

"Yeah." He shouldn't have sighed aloud. "I'd been looking forward to a burger for lunch, is all."

Rachel raised her eyebrows, clearly not believing his attempt at levity. "That's what's on your mind?"

It was now. He shrugged.

"I'm sorry, you're right. It's been a while since breakfast." She tilted her head to the side. "Have you ever had to be rescued before? Will it be much longer?"

Wouldn't hurt to distract her with some stories.

"Sure I have. Never fun waiting for backup when comms go down, but at least we aren't under fire here."

Her brows knitted together. "How long did you have to wait?"

Samuel's mind returned to the longest three hours of his life. "A while. I was in a convoy in Afghanistan, and a rocket launcher took out the vehicle in front. No warning. It was traveling in front of us, then it went up in flames. No way forward, no way back. They'd blocked our comms, so we had to dig in and wait for air support." No need to add anything about the screams and groans of the dying soldiers that haunted him to this day. "But help did come, just like help will come for us."

"Our help cometh from the Lord." Rachel's words both jarred and comforted him.

"Maybe."

"You're not a believer?"

"God and I have had a tumultuous relationship lately."

"I'm sorry to hear that." Did he imagine the judgment in her voice? "Sometimes I question the Lord for letting Sarah die." Not judgment. Compassion.

"I'm working on it, though. I've been praying more, for sure."

"That's good. I've definitely prayed more in

the last six months than all the years I've been on this earth."

"Yeah." He reached out to hold her hand, but the welcome sound of an MH-60 Jayhawk's rotors interrupted him. The coast guard had found them.

The beating blades of the helicopter sent a ripple of anxiety through Rachel. Hope dawned, along with a renewed urgency to get back safe to Katie. She was sure Samuel was holding something back about the plane. The moment he deflected her question rather than telling her she was wrong, it was obvious he suspected sabotage. Now she didn't suspect—she *knew.* Whoever had cut her brakes, shot up her house, tried to suffocate her with gas and attempted to run them off the road wouldn't stop until she was dead. So if Samuel had any suspicions, given the amount of evidence he needed to be sure, Rachel could be satisfied the suspicions would be proven true.

Which left questions. What would the perpetrator do next? How long until he knew they'd survived the plane crash? Would they be safe at the hospital? Was Katie safe with Beth? At least they'd be safe for now with the US Coast Guard. Samuel had already opened the cover and now stood to wave his arms at the approaching chopper. She tracked the rescue swimmer being lowered into the water in bright yellow-and-orange scuba gear, complete with a yellow helmet and snorkel. He unclipped and swam toward them, fast. The noise from the chopper drowned out all other sound.

Samuel grabbed her arm and raised his voice. "They'll send down a basket for you, don't worry. He's just coming over to help."

Rachel wiped her wet hair from her face, tasting salt. She didn't care how the coast guard got them out, so long as they did it quickly.

The swimmer pulled up a foot short of the life raft. His voice boomed with a welcome cheerfulness. "Hi, folks, I'm Cody. I'm from the US Coast Guard. Are you okay in there? Any injuries?"

"No, we're fine. Just cold." Samuel leaned toward him so he could hear better. "It's just the two of us."

"Let's get you out of here." Cody made a hand signal, and soon a metal cage appeared, dangling from the helicopter.

Samuel wrapped his arm around Rachel while the Jayhawk approached. Tears welled behind her eyelids. What a relief to be held safe in his arms. She turned her face into his shoulder to shelter from the spray, grateful for the protection. It'd be over soon; she just had to keep going.

Cody caught the cage and lowered it to the edge of the life raft. "You need help to climb in?"

"I've got her." Samuel helped Rachel into the cage, his strong hands steadying her when she stumbled. The TPA and life jacket cushioned her, and Cody positioned her correctly before they pulled her up. She closed her eyes on the ascent, as much to avoid watching what was happening as to keep the buffeting water out of her eyes. *Don't need to see that drop, thank you.*

The rotors swelled to a whining crescendo as she approached the belly of the beast, and she opened her eyes. Another coast guard member, with a helmet and headphones, hung attached to the ceiling of the Jayhawk by a harness. He reached to pull the cage through the door. Without a word, he hauled her out of the cage and quickly sent it back down.

A younger uniformed man smiled and helped her into a seat, gently harnessing her into place and putting headphones over her ears. "I'm Lee. How are you doing, ma'am? Cody treat you okay?"

"I'm fine, thanks. Cody did a great job."

"That your husband down there?"

Rachel shook her head, even while she imagined how nice it would be to answer with a yes. The thought made her pause. Why would she consider having a husband when she could barely take care of a child?

"He's a cop."

Lee did a double take. "You don't look like a felon."

"I'm not. He's helping me with a case."

He continued to chat, but Rachel didn't hear a word. Her mind returned to the past few hours. Alone on a life raft, freezing, near death, she wouldn't have wanted to be stuck with anyone else.

Soon, Samuel had been hauled into the chopper and they'd been strapped in. The swimmer was next, and he stowed the cage. The Jayhawk's rotors whined; it banked to the right and they accelerated away from the crash site. Hopefully, the journey would be quick. Rachel couldn't wait to be back on dry land.

Samuel took her hand in his and gave it a squeeze. The action sent a shiver through her.

He leaned toward her. "You doing okay?"

Rachel grimaced. "I'm grateful we survived."

A deep sigh whistled from his lips, and he nodded.

"You're a great pilot."

He pursed his lips. Was that a blush from her compliment? Rachel couldn't be sure. She squeezed his hand back, and he smiled.

"I don't understand what happened. You suspect sabotage, don't you?"

Samuel let go of her hand and frowned. "I think we should wait—"

"Until we're safe. Yes you said that before. But I need to know what you think *now*." Frustration rippled through her. "Danger has been following me since my brakes were cut. I just want to know who's doing this."

"I know. We're all working on that. O'Halloran is chasing up the ballistics today, probably as we speak. If this guy's slipped up, we'll find out." He grabbed her hands again, warming them.

Lee interrupted, yelling to be heard. "Our ETA is thirty-five minutes."

Rachel's stomach churned, and she was glad of Samuel's hands to steady her. Thirty-five minutes, plus however long it took to get from the US Coast Guard base to her dad's bedside. No time to release the emotions that had been building. *Lord, please help me keep it together. Help me get through the next little while for Dad's sake.* Her father needed her to remain calm in his final days…or hours. How long did he have?

Would he be awake? The doubts she'd pushed to the side while focused on survival crowded in. *What if he doesn't like me?* Tears sprang to her eyes, and she blinked rapidly.

Without giving it much thought, she leaned into Samuel and closed her eyes. He ran his thumb up and down her hand. Staying calm became a little easier with him there. She wasn't alone, and that was everything at the moment.

But a thread of fear ran through her stomach at the thought of the hours ahead. Despite what Samuel might say, she was convinced Sarah and Hank had been murdered. What if the danger followed her to the hospital?

EIGHT

An hour later, they'd reached the palliative care facility. Rachel could've done with a warm shower and a little more in her stomach, but she reminded herself to be thankful they'd made it here at all. Dry clothes and an energy bar would have to do. Not to mention the "all clear" from the US Coast Guard medic.

The walls were a light aqua, and pots of indoor plants decorated the lobby along with watercolor prints of landscapes. The faux wood-grain floor ran up to a marbled stone reception desk, where a receptionist spoke in calm, hushed tones. "Yes, ma'am, I'll transfer your call."

"I'm here to see John Bishop, I'm his daughter." The words sounded strange.

"Please take a seat. I'll call the nurse." The receptionist dialed, but her voice faded into the background when Rachel caught a glimpse of her reflection. She grimaced, her heart racing. The sparkling-clean one-way glass behind the receptionist revealed her shameful appearance.

What would her father think of her? He hadn't seen her for over twenty years, and his first impression would be of her looking like she'd been on a ten-day wet-weather trek.

"Are you okay?" Samuel hadn't fared much better, but the rumpled look suited him. Rugged, unshaven, briny. While not conventionally handsome, something about him flooded her with warmth.

"Nervous."

He squeezed her shoulder and led her to a seat. "I'm right here."

She clasped her hands together and worked through what she wanted to say to her father. Would he even be awake? The hunger she'd felt left her. Did he know about Sarah? Her mom? Would she have to break the news that they were both dead? Would he even care? The thought shot through her like an electrical charge. He hadn't bothered to find them when they were adults, no longer subject to court orders. He seemed to want to see her. Why hadn't he called earlier?

"Rachel Harding?" She startled when a nurse interrupted her thoughts. The woman's face had that somber look she'd seen before. When the police officer came to her door with the news of Sarah and Hank.

"Yes, I'm Rachel."

"Come with me, please."

They followed the nurse, who led them down

a hall and into a side room. No beds, just some comfortable chairs.

"Take a seat."

Rachel frowned and stood in the doorway. "I'd like to see my father as soon as possible, please. Can we have the intake interview or whatever this is after?"

The nurse held out her hand, gesturing to a chair. Her face changed to a patient, melancholy look that Rachel couldn't read. "This isn't about paperwork."

Her skin prickled. She wanted to run away, but she sat. "I'm sorry, Rachel, your father passed an hour ago." The nurse's voice overflowed with compassion.

Rachel's body slumped, and numbness swept over her. She couldn't speak, couldn't respond.

Samuel reached over and squeezed her hand. "I'm so sorry, Rachel."

She couldn't even look at him. Nothing made sense. How could the Lord be so cruel? To give her hope, then snatch it away.

"I'll lcavc you alone." The nurse stood, and the action snapped Rachel back into the room.

"Can I see him?"

"Sure you can. He's still in his room."

Samuel helped her up, and she leaned against him while they walked over to the elevator. The nurse pressed the button to the third floor, and they ascended in silence.

At least I didn't tell Katie. The little girl couldn't do with more loss in her life. They'd sweep this away without her even knowing her grandfather had existed. *More lies.* No, she wouldn't be like her mother. She'd tell Katie. Eventually. Once she grew up and Rachel had gotten to the bottom of what had happened.

They reached the room, and the nurse paused at the door. "Would you like me to come in with you?"

Rachel didn't know how to respond. Did it matter?

Samuel squeezed her arm. "We'll be fine, thanks."

The nurse left, and Samuel turned to Rachel, hand remaining on her shoulder. "You don't have to do this now if you don't want to."

Rachel sighed. "Yes, I do." She opened the door.

The room displayed the same color scheme as the rest of the place—aqua and apricot beige. Her skin tingled with discomfort when the familiar smell of antiseptic hit her.

A man—her father—lay peacefully in the bed, his head resting on a pillow. If she didn't know better, she'd guess he was napping.

Rachel sat in the chair next to the bed and took him in. His face didn't resemble the photo. The plumpness had been replaced with gaunt jaundice. His hair had lost its body, the thin, gray remains pasted against his head. *I'll never see his eyes. I'll never talk to him.* Someone may have failed to kill her, but they'd stolen those last precious moments from her.

The heaviness of it all became too much, and her head dropped into her hands. She couldn't hold back her emotions anymore. She'd lost her father. Again. Although she'd mourned this man her whole childhood, she'd start the grieving all over once more. Worse, today she'd have no comfort from the lies her mother had told. The curtain had been pulled back. Her father had been accessible to her for her entire life. And she'd been moments too late.

Rachel sobbed, unable to stop. Samuel's hand rubbing her back didn't help, but it didn't hurt, either. While glad he was here with her, she was also a bit ashamed for him to see her come so unglued. Then again, what did it matter?

"Rachel." Samuel's voice sounded firm. "We should get out of here."

Rachel wanted to scream, *What's the rush?* This would be the last memory she'd have of her father. She glanced at him, barely able to see for the tears. "I can't go yet." Her voice rasped, unrecognizable.

Samuel gently wiped her eyes with a tissue. "I know it's been a terrible shock, but you're going to get through this."

"No, I won't." She took another tissue and blew her nose. "My own father didn't wait for me."

He took her hands in his. "That is not on you."

"I want to stay. Just a little longer."

"This past week has been rough, but I've seen just how courageous and selfless you are. I admire that, and I understand your pain. But you have Katie to think about now. We need to get back. We need to find out who wants *you* dead."

His eyes searched hers. Deep brown and soft, like fine suede. He'd removed the snow jacket, and the sleeves from the borrowed shirt rode up his arms, revealing the strong, sinewy muscles of his forearms. His rough hands absently massaged hers.

"Okay. But first I want to talk to the nurse. She must know more about my father."

Samuel's mind raced while he led Rachel to the nurses' station. Had he been too harsh? Should he have left her to sob for longer? He hated to see a woman cry, especially Rachel. Not only that, but he also knew that once grief took hold, there was nothing to do but wait until it passed. Memories of his mother's death fought for attention. How would he have felt if someone had pulled him away from his grief? Maybe they should have.

Rachel didn't have time for hers, not with the perpetrator willing to drop their floatplane from the sky. Someone with that skill level presented a greater danger than he'd first thought. Someone with basic mechanical knowledge could locate and tamper with a brake cable on a minivan. But downing a plane midflight? Wouldn't take long for them to figure out Rachel had survived. Samuel had to find the guy, and fast.

The nurse who'd taken them into John Bishop's room held out two cups of coffee. "Here, why don't you sit down and we can go through next steps."

She led them to an alcove, the smell of coffee wafting after her. Samuel waited for Rachel to choose a seat, then sat next to her. A box sat on the side table, and the nurse picked it up, handing it to Rachel.

"Here's your father's personal effects. He asked us to dispose of the contents, but you may like to keep something."

Rachel's face dropped, and she clutched the box to her chest. "I can't believe he didn't think to leave them for me."

Samuel shared her surprise. The man had known Rachel would come. Maybe there was something he was missing. Perhaps when the court documents came back, there would be a clearer picture.

The nurse pursed her lips and swallowed. She glanced at Samuel, then back at Rachel. "I'm sorry. Sometimes people at the end of their life can behave in unexpected ways. How about I leave you with the box and I'll come back to check on you soon." She rushed back to the nurses' station.

Rachel's chin trembled. "Can you believe this?"

Her hands fumbled the lid from the box, and Samuel took it for her, placing it to one side. "Maybe there'll be answers in here," he said.

Rachel pulled a framed picture from the top. "Must've been taken a year or two earlier, when he wasn't sick." She turned it so Samuel could see, too.

Rachel studied the picture, running her thumb over the ornate gilt edge of the frame. John Bishop smiled for the camera, shaking hands with another businessman. "Who's this? Some business colleague? I don't even know what my father did for a living." She rubbed her forehead.

Samuel couldn't bear to see her like this. "How about we look through the rest of the papers."

She placed the photo to one side and lifted the next photo out of the box. Her father and a woman, taken at least thirty years ago, if the fashion and hair styles were accurate. The oval frame must've been a similar age to the photo; the gilt on parts of the floral detail had worn off. "Do you think this is my dad's first wife? Do you think she's still alive too?"

Samuel shrugged. No use getting her hopes up. "If she were alive, wouldn't he have a later photo?"

Rachel sighed. "You're probably right." She flicked through the box. "There's no pictures of Mom, or Sarah and me."

"Does he have any official papers in there? A will?"

Rachel handed him the box. "Have at it. I need to clear my head." She stood and stretched. "I'm going to find a bathroom."

"Okay, I'll be right here." Samuel kept an eye on her as she walked to the ladies' room, then returned his gaze to the box. Among the photos were documents, files, letters, and small boxes that might contain jewelry or other personal effects. He undid the tarnished brass snap closure on the front of the first box. A yellow-gold wedding and engagement ring set. The diamond on the engagement ring was princess cut, at least three carats. The set looked old, well-worn. No engravings or other identifying marks on the rings. Nothing printed on the velvet and satin-lined leather box. Samuel frowned and opened the small emerald green leather box. A ladies' Rolex watch encrusted with diamonds. Who did these belong to? Rachel's mother, perhaps. Rachel probably wouldn't recognize them, anyway.

The nurse approached. "Are you doing okay? Where's Miss Harding?"

"Restroom. Say, did anyone come to visit Mr. Bishop today?"

The nurse paused, perhaps thrown by the question. "I don't know. My shift only started an hour ago."

"Is there someone I can talk with who would know?"

"I'll call my supervisor." The nurse turned to go, then turned back. "I almost forgot. Here are the details of Mr. Bishop's attorney. Maybe she can help?" She passed them to Samuel, then walked back to the nurses' station. The paper had a phone number and an address. Samuel's phone hadn't survived the plane crash, and he felt lost without it. They'd have to get new phones as soon as they returned to Cordova.

Rachel returned from the bathroom. The puffiness from her crying jag had settled. She must've used some cold water.

"Did you find anything?" she asked. "A will?"

"I didn't get that far." He swallowed. "Did your mom keep her wedding ring?"

Rachel rubbed her eyebrows. "Um, yeah. I still have it. Why?"

No use holding anything back. He opened the box with the ring set and handed it to her. "Not your mom's?"

"Huh?" She shook her head. "This is from my father's things? It must be his first wife's, I guess. Maybe you were right, then, about the woman in the photo dying. Unless they got a divorce." She reached into the box and drew out a file. "Guess we should keep looking." Then she pulled a notebook from the box and opened it. Handwritten journal entries.

A woman approached. "I'm Nancy Kean, the supervisor. I understand you've been asking about Mr. Bishop?"

Samuel stood. "Yes. Has he had any visitors today? Anyone over the past couple of weeks?"

"Why do you ask?" Nancy's tone seemed pleasant but had a defensive edge Samuel didn't like.

"He asked you to dispose of this box, but there's at least six figures worth of jewelry inside. We're trying to establish whether he has any other living relatives."

Rachel gasped. "That much?"

Nancy licked her lips, then swallowed. "You obviously didn't know him very well. Mr. Bishop ran oil rigs up in Prudhoe Bay. Passed down from his father before him. Six figures would be a drop in the ocean for him."

"But all of these jewels and photos…" Rachel's eyebrows drew together. "He knew I was coming, but he just wanted to dispose of them?"

"He didn't strike me as the sentimental type. Look, take it with you and we'll consider it disposed of. Is there anything else you need?"

Rachel's shoulders drooped, and Samuel's heart ached for her. If her father had oil money, she shouldn't be struggling financially, and her mother shouldn't have, either. The mystery of Rachel's family had drawn him in, and he wanted to get to the bottom of it. Nancy must know more.

"Yes. I'd like to ask you some more questions, if that's convenient." He paused, glancing at Rachel. "On Rachel's behalf."

Rachel's stomach lurched when she saw the time. "I really need to check in with my niece before she goes to bed. I promised I'd call her after dinner. Is there a phone I can use? My phone is..." *At the bottom of Prince William Sound.* "Not available."

"Sure, just go down to the lobby. There's an outside line you can use free of charge."

"I'll come with you." Samuel seemed distracted, his eyes on Nancy.

Nancy cleared her throat. "I have to go in ten minutes."

"It's fine. I'll meet you in the lobby." Rachel forced a smile in Samuel's direction, then walked down the hall and around the corner toward the elevator.

The whole situation felt surreal.

Rachel stepped into the empty elevator. Something moved behind her, and when she turned to check, a searing pain shot through the back of her scalp.

Her head spun, and she struggled to control her breathing as she sprawled on the floor of the elevator. The blow had made her woozy but hadn't knocked her out. She wanted to gasp for air. Open her eyes. But she had enough sense to pretend she'd been whacked unconscious. She'd get hit again if he thought he'd failed. Whoever he was.

All Rachel knew for sure was this must be the man who'd tried to kill her. Who'd succeeded in killing Sarah and Hank. And she was trapped in an elevator with him. How had he found her so quickly?

If he thought she was out cold, it might buy her time to escape. The door dinged, and he picked her up, flinging her over his shoulder. The movement made the throb of her head worse. His hands were strong and bony and painfully tight around her legs. The coarse polyester of his jacket scratched her cheek. *Where are you, Samuel?*

The man stepped out from the elevator, grunting, and Rachel risked opening her eyes a crack. Not in the foyer. Somewhere dark. The basement? Assuming there was a basement. Samuel might never find her! *Lord, please send help, or at least show me what to do.*

Rachel opened her eyes again.

Automatic lights flicked on, illuminating the space and the rows of cars. Didn't that supervisor say she would soon finish her shift? If Rachel could get away, Nancy would be down here soon, wouldn't she? She could scare the man away.

The man coughed and pressed a key fob. He *did* plan to put her in the trunk. It didn't make sense, though. He'd gone to such great pains to make things look accidental up until now. Had he given up on that? Or did he have something else in mind?

Rachel knew if her abductor successfully managed to get her into the trunk of his car, her chances of survival were low. Adrenaline surged through her, making her stomach rock hard. No way would she give up without a fight. *I have to get away.*

NINE

Samuel's gut clenched. He had to question Nancy, but he couldn't let Rachel go anywhere alone. She'd already walked off down the hallway. Why hadn't she waited for him? Probably wasn't thinking straight, after all that had happened. Her vulnerability left him with a sense of unease. He crossed his arms.

"I'll need your cell number for follow-up questions."

Nancy pursed her lips. "You can reach me here on the landline."

"Only when you're here."

"When I'm not here, I'm *not* on the clock."

Samucl gritted his teeth. "You do realize that Rachel is involved in an investigation?" Nancy didn't have to know the investigation didn't officially include Rachel's father.

"You have a badge?"

He pulled the water-logged badge from his jacket. They were built to last.

Nancy raised an eyebrow with mild surprise.

"Sorry, Officer. Of course, I'll help in any way I can." She handed him a business card, looking anything but sorry.

"Thanks." He tucked the business card and the paper with the lawyer's details into the box, then took off down the hall after Rachel.

The elevator doors had only just closed, and he pressed the button. Hopefully, it'd open up again. Not this time. He scoffed and headed to the stairs.

Heart pounding from the exertion, Samuel reached the foyer and stood in front of the elevator. Rachel should've been here by now. He surveyed the area, taking in the front door and the receptionist. Nothing seemed out of place. He pressed the elevator button, his legs restless. If only Bruce were with him—the dog had a sixth sense for where to go. The elevator door opened, empty. His stomach knotted. Where was she?

He considered the facts. The elevator had gone down, not up—there was no *up*. Rachel could've gotten off on the second floor by mistake. Not likely; the receptionist was visible from the elevator. Rachel would realize her mistake.

He rushed to the receptionist, placing the box of John Bishop's belongings on the counter. "Did you see Rachel?"

The woman held up a finger with a phone held to her ear. Samuel's jaw clenched with frustration. He looked around.

He rushed back to the elevator and pressed the

button. The elevator hadn't moved, and the doors opened. He glanced inside, blocking the doors from closing. There were four buttons—*3, 2, 1, LL*. Why hadn't he noticed that before? That's what he got for being distracted.

The receptionist had finished with her call. "I haven't seen her, I'm sorry."

Samuel pressed the *LL* button. Nothing happened. "Do I need a pass for the lower level?"

"Yes, sir."

Before he could question her further, the phone rang, and the receptionist answered the call.

Samuel growled with frustration. If Rachel had exited on the well-populated second floor, she'd be fine. But in the basement? She wouldn't have traveled there alone. No time to get his own elevator pass. He rushed back to the stairs.

Taking them two at a time, he reached the fire door to the basement and swung it open. The sound of a yell and a grunt greeted him.

"Help!" Rachel screamed.

"Rachel!" Samuel sprinted toward her voice, meeting her as she stumbled toward him.

A car door slammed, its engine roared to life, and the vehicle sped to the exit. He resisted the urge to race after it. Even at his fastest, he wouldn't reach it in time. Without a radio or a firearm, he had to focus on getting Rachel to safety.

Rachel clung to him, gasping for air, eyes wide. Blood trickled down her neck. More important than catching the assailant was Rachel's safety.

"You're hurt. What happened?"

She reached for the back of her head, and her hand came back with blood. "He tried to knock me out."

Protective anger welled within him, and his muscles quivered. He wrapped his arm around Rachel. "I got you." If only he had his radio. Backup. Anything. "Did you see him?"

"Not his face, but he was tall and thin. Taller than you. He thought I was unconscious, so when he tried to put me in the trunk, I made him overbalance. He let go and I kicked him and ran." Tears spilled down her cheeks, and he wiped them away with his thumb before he could think. Her gaze mesmerized him, the artificial light turning her eyes gray, almost steel blue.

"You did great, Rachel."

The lights in the basement went out, and Rachel stepped back with a gasp. The movement triggered the lights, which flicked back on.

Her eyes widened. "I still need to call Katie."

"Let's find some phones. You can do that while I arrange for a flight home. Then you can tell me all the details."

Several hours later, Samuel's mind raced while the plane left the tarmac, ascending on its way from Anchorage to Cordova. They'd decided to fly commercial, as much for his peace of mind as Rachel's. Rather than find a hotel, they'd stayed at the airport for what was left of the night. Rachel had snoozed on and off, and Samuel remained wide awake. Now she sat next to the window, her hands clasped in her lap. It baffled him that she seemed so calm after what had happened. Had she gone into shock?

Her conversation with Katie had been short, interrupting some activity or other Beth had organized. Another uneventful day for them at school, further cementing Samuel's feeling that Katie wasn't a target.

The surveillance cameras from the hospital didn't have great coverage, but there was enough to show a tall, thin man wearing a baseball cap, generic maintenance clothes and work gloves enter the elevator. Just as Rachel had described, and matching the physical qualities of the man on the dirt bike. He walked with purpose, no hesitation. Nothing good enough for facial recognition. No chance of fingerprints. The receptionist vaguely remembered him coming in the door—they had a lot of maintenance men come and go—but didn't recall him requesting a parking pass. Besides, the passes were unsophisticated, so they couldn't glean whether someone had given it to him or he'd stolen it. Putting out a BOLO for a tall, thin man didn't seem like progress.

Samuel longed to hold Rachel, guard her from the man who'd necessitated the bandage on her head.

She turned to catch him staring. "I'm not a city girl." He must've given her a blank stare, because she smiled with embarrassment. "What I mean is, being in Anchorage even for a day has made me appreciate the quiet of Cordova. I don't think I could live in a city again."

"I don't miss the city, either."

"You worked in the city before you came here?"

He resisted the urge to tuck a loose strand of hair behind her ear. "Not a major city, but yeah, Mayfield's bigger than Cordova."

"Mayfield, Kentucky? Close to home?"

Close to Amanda. "I've always been a country boy at heart."

"Why did you leave?"

Samuel's thoughts scrambled. Such a personal question.

He swallowed. "It's a long story."

She shrugged and gestured around the half-empty flight. "We've got time." When he didn't reply, she frowned. "You don't have to tell me if you don't want to." A tinge of hurt echoed in her voice. After the past few days, what they'd been through, she deserved his confidence. She could make her own judgments about him.

"I suffered a loss," he said. That didn't begin to explain it.

Sympathy filled Rachel's eyes, and she reached for his hand, her fingers slightly cold. "I'm so sorry."

If anyone understood loss, it was Rachel. She'd lost both parents, her sister and her brother-in-law. He'd lost his mother and the woman he'd loved.

But she hadn't caused any of what she'd lost. He, on the other hand… "It was my fault. Amanda died because of me."

She gave him a skeptical look. "What happened?"

Samuel closed his eyes. He didn't want to talk or think about it. The memories filled his dreams and a lot of his waking thoughts. A squeeze of her hand on his spurred him on.

"We were at a gas station during an armed robbery."

The short explanation didn't begin to describe the reality of what had happened. How could Samuel put into words the tragic circumstances without reliving the pain?

Rachel lifted her hand to his cheek, her fingers now warm from his hand. "Who was Amanda?"

He forced himself to meet her eyes. "My fiancée. Amanda was the widow of my best friend, Jeff. You know that ambush I told you about?"

"Yes."

"He died in that. He had a little girl, Isabel. He made me promise I'd take care of them." The words stuck in his throat. "It'd been a hot day, and Amanda and Isabel decided to come into the gas station while I paid so they could buy ice cream. While they were deciding on which flavors to choose, a gunman entered the store." Samuel lowered his chin to his chest. The shame of what happened next haunted him. "I tried to talk the guy down, but he didn't want to talk."

"That's awful." She licked her lips, as if looking for the right words. "Did you catch the guy?"

"He died at the scene. I shot him. But not before he pulled the trigger. His firearm was automatic, and it sprayed bullets all over the place. They ricocheted everywhere. That's what killed her. The ricochet."

That one tragic burst of gunfire had left his faith in tatters. The memory of Isabel's screams while Amanda died in his arms remained painfully fresh. Thankfully, the little girl had remained physically unharmed.

"I'm so sorry for your loss." She pursed her lips. "I don't understand how you're responsible, though."

Samuel drew a deep breath. "I should've taken a shot when I had it. I hesitated. Thought I could talk him down." *Stupid.*

"You were alone?"

"I was off duty." Thankfully, he always carried a sidearm. The investigation found his actions prevented more loss of life, that he was a selfless hero, but none of that mattered to Samuel. He was no hero.

"I had my back to the door. I saw him too late." He'd pushed Amanda and Isabel to the floor and rushed to confront the gunman. They should've been safe there. Samuel stared past Rachel, Prince William Sound now in view. Why had they been spared when Amanda had not?

Did he dare tell Rachel the shock waves he'd created in the wake of the tragedy? May as well. "My mother died soon after. It's possible—probable—my actions hastened her death."

Rachel's eyes widened. Though her lips parted, she didn't speak.

Samuel's heart contracted painfully. "I handled the whole situation badly. Instead of staying in the community, I bailed out. Isabel had gone to live with Amanda's parents in Texas, and I didn't see any reason to stay. It broke my mother's heart, losing Amanda and Isabel, then me leaving. She'd been battling cancer and died a few months later. My dad blames me for it. He thinks the stress killed her. I don't think he'll ever forgive me for it. Doubt my brothers will, either." He didn't dare look at Rachel, imagining the horror and disgust that must be written on her face.

A warm hand gently squeezed his. "I'm so sorry you lost your mom. But I doubt your family blames you for her death. You were grieving. I lost my mind a little when Mom died. Made some bad decisions. Sarah helped me through that." She sighed. "Honestly, more than six months on, I can barely get through each day with her gone. If it weren't for Katie, I probably wouldn't get out of bed. You may have left, but you kept going. You've come to Cordova and done a lot of good."

He turned. Rather than disgust, a deep sadness and understanding filled her eyes. She continued, "If there's one thing I've learned these past few months, it's that we're not in control. I doubt you could've done anything differently, and even if you had, the outcome might've been the same. I hope one day you can see that."

Samuel didn't believe it. He knew in his heart of hearts that if only he'd taken the shot, Amanda would still be alive today. And maybe his mom would've kept fighting.

The lump in Rachel's throat felt like a stone, and the pain relief the hospice nurse had given her made her lightheaded. How could she process what Samuel had just told her without bursting into tears? He'd been through so much, and now he'd been saddled with her and Katie—a recurring nightmare situation.

Samuel was an incredible man. Whether she meant to or not, she'd opened her heart to him. But she sensed he couldn't do the same. Not if he couldn't forgive himself. The specter of guilt hanging over him must be all-consuming. If he couldn't open his heart to his own family, how could he open it to her? The jumble of emotions was almost too much. *Lord, please help me keep it together.*

She drew a deep breath. Remembered her own insight—she was not in control. The Lord had a plan. Even if He'd taken her family, He'd given her Katie. The thought of the emotional energy it would take to include Samuel in her life weighed her down until she could barely breathe. Katie's well-being was all she had room for, and that should be her focus.

Would she have to plan her father's funeral? She'd planned Sarah's and Hank's by herself. Barely made it through. When she got back home, had a phone, she'd go through the box of possessions and work out who to call. Maybe there'd be a personal assistant who knew more.

The flight lasted less than an hour, and Rachel and Samuel hadn't even unclipped their seat belts. She settled back in her seat and stared out the window, where the early-morning sun reflected like a menacing aura over Orca Inlet. Her mouth grew dry at the thought of the tall, thin man in the baseball cap. Would he be waiting for them? Seemed unlikely, unless he'd taken this flight. Or he had access to his own plane. The only way in or out of Cordova was by sea or air. Rachel sighed.

"Are you okay?" Samuel's voice held the same softness from back in the basement parking garage. But now wasn't the time to think about it. *Keep it together.*

"I'm okay." She smiled. "Guess you're looking forward to seeing Bruce as much as I am Katie."

"Yeah, it'll be good to get back home."

Back home. Because Cordova was starting to become home. Despite the danger, this was Katie's home, and Samuel's home. They weren't going anywhere, and neither would she.

It wasn't until they got out of the taxi at Beth's house that Rachel realized Samuel wasn't carrying the box of her father's belongings.

"I left it at the reception desk." Samuel's distress melted the harsh words she'd almost spoken.

"It's okay."

Samuel shook his head. "I'm sorry, Rachel, I'll get them to courier it to the station."

They walked toward Beth's house. "Do you think Beth will let us stay another night? I feel like we're overstaying our welcome."

Before Samuel could reply, the front door burst open, and Katie and Bruce rushed toward them.

"Aunt Rachel!" Katie slammed into her and wrapped her arms around Rachel's legs. Rachel's heart swelled with love for the little girl. "Come see my painting! It's your favorite colors!" She stopped and looked up. "What happened to your head?"

"It got hurt."

"Oh no. Is it sore?"

"A little. I'll be fine." Katie nodded, satisfied. Rachel relaxed, glad she'd rehearsed the answer during the plane trip.

Bruce's tail thwacked the backs of her knees, and she glanced toward Samuel. He'd crouched to Bruce's level, eyes crinkled closed to avoid Bruce's enthusiastic licks. He laughed. "Nice to see you, too, boy. Okay, that's enough." He stood and smiled at Beth. His face had lost its tension, and longing rushed through Rachel, dulling her senses. How she wished things could be different. That she and Samuel could have a future.

Beth smiled warmly. "Good timing. Jock O'Halloran just dropped Bruce over. Did you have a good trip?" They'd agreed to wait to tell her what had happened.

Katie tugged on Rachel's arm, saving her from answering. "Come on, you're going to love it."

Rachel followed Katie toward the front door, and everyone else followed.

"See? It's you, me, Bruce and Samuel!" The

picture had been carefully painted with the details of the house, Bruce's collar, Samuel's uniform and even Rachel's favorite sweater. Katie stood resplendent in pink frills and aspirational floor-length hair.

A weight filled her chest. They looked like a family. "That's beautiful, honey." Did Katie think they could be a family? Even if that were possible, someone was trying to prevent it from ever happening.

It took a moment before Rachel realized Beth was speaking. "There's a note to call the station. You can use my phone." She handed the phone and note to Samuel, who took a few paces into the hallway.

Katie tugged Rachel's sleeve. "It's our house! I drew it just like that picture on Mommy's desk." Sarah had nurtured a love for art in Katie with as much care as Hank had her love of the natural environment.

"I see that, Kitty-cat. Look at all that lovely green grass. It's summer?"

Katie grinned. "Yep."

They'd have to survive winter first. A chill ran through her at the thought.

Samuel touched her arm, and she turned. "Everything okay?"

"Yeah." He hesitated, then smiled. "Better than okay. O'Halloran checked the DMV information against everyone who flew in and out of Cordova in the past two days. There was a handful who fit the profile, but only one who could have committed every crime. They're picking him up now." His smile broadened. "I think we got him."

Rachel closed her eyes with relief. But her throat thickened as a whispered question remained. Why did this man want her dead?

TEN

Samuel strode into the police station with Bruce at his heels. His muscles tensed when he thought about the man he had to interview. Thankfully, he'd been taken into custody, and Samuel could leave Rachel without fear. But what that man had done to her, the pain he'd caused—both physical and psychological—stirred anger Samuel didn't want to feel. He had to keep his cool. As if sensing his master's emotions, Bruce nuzzled his hand and huffed.

"Okay, boy, I get it. I'm no use to anyone if I make this personal." Samuel ruffled Bruce between the ears.

He dumped his coat at his desk and grabbed a pen and notepad, then walked over to the interview room.

Jock O'Halloran sat with the suspect, the door ajar. Samuel stationed Bruce outside the door, drew a deep breath, then peered through the door and motioned for O'Halloran to come out.

The suspect didn't glance up, his gaze fixed

on his cuffed hands on the desk in front of him. He sure looked like the grainy image of the man on the surveillance camera footage. Tall, thin, wearing clothes that could pass for a maintenance worker. Someone capable of hitting Rachel over the head. Samuel unclenched his fists. Professional, not personal.

O'Halloran grabbed the file and walked into the hallway. He shut the door and handed the file to Samuel. "Donal Hayne, charter pilot. He has visitation rights with his children here in Cordova on a weekly basis. Based on your timeline, he's been here for every incident. The flight records confirm it. He even flew out yesterday morning before you did and returned yesterday evening. He has mechanical skills—could've cut that brake line."

A charter pilot would have a good knowledge of floatplanes, too, including how to sabotage them. Certainly had access.

"You've Mirandized him?"

"Yeah, he's asked for his lawyer. Hasn't said anything else."

Samuel clenched his jaw. So much for his plan to get a confession. They'd have to rely on the evidence they had.

"How long will that be?"

"She's flying out from Anchorage, so it could be a while. Although it's a charter, so at least it'll be today."

"Do we have anything more than circumstantial evidence?"

"Not yet, but we're going over his movements in detail. We'll interview witnesses, which should give us more, and I've requested his phone records."

Samuel cleared his throat. "You've done a great job, O'Halloran. Especially that expedited warrant."

Jock swallowed, seemingly uncomfortable with the praise. "How's Rachel doing?"

His heart skipped at the mention of her name. "She's tired but happy we caught the guy." Samuel didn't mention the painful wound on her head that meant she wouldn't get a good night's sleep. He'd left her to pack up Katie's things, ready to return to their house. Beth had taken Katie to school, so hopefully, Rachel could get some rest.

"I'll take Bruce for a walk. Call me if she arrives when I'm gone." It'd give Samuel a chance to clear his head before the interview.

"No problem. Here, boy." O'Halloran slipped Bruce a treat, and the dog gobbled it down in one gulp.

The chill in the air felt more intense than it had the day before. The rainstorm had brought with it an even icier breeze that buffeted the boats in the marina. He and Bruce looped back around and headed toward Eyak Lake.

"You want a walk, boy?" Samuel hadn't interviewed the charter company himself. No question O'Halloran was a fine police officer, and he trusted his work, but Samuel's plane had gone down. Sometimes a personal touch could lever out a little more information.

Twenty minutes later, the charter owner, Tim Flynn, looked up from his desk, cup of coffee in hand. "Bruce!"

To Bruce's credit, he remained in place next to Samuel—the only indication the dog had heard the greeting was his tail and the enormous grin on his face.

Samuel smiled and released Bruce, who bounded over to Tim for a pat. "Greetings like that can make a man feel like chopped liver."

Tim chuckled. "Honestly, I'm glad you're in one piece. I've been tied up here, but I planned to come by once the last charter lands. Check on how you're all doing. Terrible business."

O'Halloran had taken great pains to steer clear of the sabotage angle when he'd interviewed Tim. As far as Tim knew, it'd been a mechanical fault. He'd taken the list of people who had been on the premises in the twenty-four hours prior as a matter of routine.

Samuel waved away the excuse. "Hopefully, the insurance will cover it."

"With the premiums I pay, it'd better! Can I offer you a coffee? Just made a pot."

"Sure."

Tim walked over to the coffee machine and reached for a mug. “Creamer?”

Samuel shook his head.

“I truly am torn up about what happened, Samuel.” He passed Samuel the mug, and wisps of steam wafted toward him. “You know I check all my planes before they go out. The assessor will try and recover it to find out what happened. Like I said, thank God you’re all right. And that poor woman, as if she hasn’t been through enough lately.” Samuel ground his teeth at the thought of Rachel’s suffering.

“I had a look at your list of persons who came around the day before. Didn’t recognize some of them. You know Donal Hayne well? I haven’t heard of him.” Samuel sipped his coffee.

Tim frowned. “I’m surprised. He’s here semiregularly, most weeks comes in. Always trying to convince me to join him for an evening of poker, or canasta, or whatever’s his flavor of the month. I’m not a gambler myself.” He scratched his head. “Charters a few planes now and then, but far as I know, he usually works out of Prudhoe Bay chartering the FIFO workers. Not many of them live here. Anyone else you don’t know?”

There were a lot of fly-in, fly-out workers throughout the region. Hayne must be busy. Samuel would have to check all flight manifests to make sure the suspect didn’t alibi out.

Satisfied Tim seemed oblivious to any nefariousness on Hayne's part, Samuel went through a few more names he didn't recognize. Nothing out of the ordinary. Looked like Donal Hayne was their guy.

He and Bruce walked down the road, and Tim called out after them. "Hold up." He jogged toward them, and Samuel waited for him to catch up.

"I forgot, one of the men *was* local, in the past. Donal Hayne. He mentioned once that he'd lived opposite Eyak Lake, up near the Lawrence place, for a time. Not sure if that's relevant? The rest of them were definitely not locals, though. Lower forty-eight mostly, and one from Nome."

Samuel's gut dropped. Donal Hayne had lived right near where Rachel now resided. No wonder he knew the area.

A few hours later, the lawyer arrived—a flashy woman in an expensive pantsuit.

"I'm Harriet Callinan, I need a moment with my client prior to the interview." Her New York accent surprised him, and the name seemed familiar. Where had he heard it before? Had she transplanted to Anchorage, or was she there on other business and this case had come up?

"No problem, take your time." Samuel showed her to the interview room and shut the door behind her.

O'Halloran smoothed his hair. "He must have money if he can afford the likes of her."

Samuel pursed his lips. A charter pilot indentured to his wife for alimony and child support for their three kids wouldn't normally have the means to fly in a city lawyer and pay her exorbitant fee. Must be something he'd missed.

This morning, he'd quizzed Rachel. She hadn't heard of anyone named Donal Hayne, and she didn't recognize him when shown his mug shot.

Samuel turned to O'Halloran. "What's his motive? Rachel hasn't set eyes on him before. What's the connection?"

O'Halloran shrugged. "Maybe he'd been stalking her or something?"

The idea didn't sit right with Samuel. Rachel would recognize him—stalkers made contact well before they started to escalate to attempted murder. "We have to dig deeper. He was born in Anchorage, so he's not local. But he raised his family here until the divorce. Before he got married, he lived locally too—near Rachel's place. His wife works part-time at the grocery store. How did he know Sarah and Hank? Did he work with them? Did they live up near the lake at the same time? Had Sarah been friends with his wife? We need to find out." Maybe Rachel would find something at home. He'd call around after the interview.

The lawyer came back to find them. "We're ready for you."

O'Halloran and Samuel stood together and

followed Ms. Callinan into the interview room. Donal Hayne remained in the same position they'd left him, only now he appeared more stooped, his eyes dull. What had his lawyer said to him?

O'Halloran turned on the tape and went through the relevant dates and Donal's whereabouts.

To each question, he responded the same: "No comment." His voice was monotone, his eye contact nonexistent.

Samuel took over. "How do you know Rachel Harding?"

"No comment."

"Did you know Hank Lawrence?"

Donal stiffened. "No comment." The slight pause before he answered told Samuel all he needed to know. Hank *was* a connection, if not *the* connection. But why Rachel? Any beef Donal might have had with Hank surely died with him. Didn't matter—Hank was a lead. They'd have to look closer into Hank's affairs for that connection.

"Did you kill Hank and Sarah Lawrence?"

Donal's face fell. "I—"

The lawyer interrupted. "Are you going to charge my client?"

O'Halloran glanced at Samuel. "Yes, the DA will be charging your client. He'll be arraigned first thing Monday."

The lawyer nodded as if satisfied, then stood. "I'll see you at the arraignment." She touched Donal Hayne on the shoulder, and he flinched.

"Hold on, we have more questions." O'Halloran's brow furrowed.

"You can question him further once he's charged."

Samuel wondered what had prompted the flinch from Donal Hayne. Did the lawyer really act in her client's best interests?

"I'll walk you out." Samuel gestured for Bruce to stay and followed Ms. Callinan to the front entrance. "What's a New Yorker doing here in little ole Cordova?"

She paused at the threshold, buttoning her expensive-looking coat and pulling on soft leather gloves. "You think this is my first rodeo? Leave the questions for the next interview."

He shrugged. "I meant no offense, ma'am. We just don't get many city folks around here unless they're tourists."

She paused, looking him up and down. Perhaps checking whether he meant what he said. She rubbed her hands together. "Probably the same reason as you, farm boy."

Something fishy was going on, but Samuel knew when he was beat. "See you Monday, ma'am."

The lawyer nodded and walked to the waiting cab. She might not have told him anything, but she'd shown him either Donal Hayne wasn't who everyone thought he was or someone else was involved.

Rachel slumped onto the sofa, her body weighed down with fatigue. Rubbing her scratchy eyes, she tried to get her eyesight back to normal. Whether the knock to the head or the lack of sleep was responsible for her blurred vision, she didn't know. Thankfully, her and Katie's belongings stood packed and waiting next to the front door for Samuel to pick them up. She'd have to organize a new car once the insurance came through. Closing her eyes, she fought the overwhelming sense of foreboding that nestled in her stomach like a visitor who'd overstayed their welcome.

She'd survived. The perpetrator—Donal Hayne—waited in custody. Katie remained safe at school. No reason to feel foreboding. *Now, rest.*

Hours later, she awoke, groggy, her head pounding. No, the pounding came from something else this time. Her heart scampered momentarily, until she remembered it couldn't be Donal Hayne. Must be Samuel at the door.

Levering her body up from the sofa took more effort than usual, her muscles stiff and sore. But she made it down the hall before Samuel had time to worry.

His smile rippled through her like a warm embrace. "Did you get a chance to rest?"

"Yeah, thanks." The sun shone low in the sky behind him. Must have been later than she thought. "We need to pick up Katie soon."

Bruce woofed. Did he recognize Katie's name? She'd be delighted.

"All taken care of. She'll be dropped back off at your place by an officer." He grabbed the bags as if they weighed nothing, and the welcome aroma of his aftershave wafted toward her. "Come on, let's get you home to your own bed."

Rachel didn't correct him. But when she thought about her own bed, it was still the one back in Missouri, in storage. Languishing along with the apartment she really needed to get around to selling. Cordova might be turning into home, but there was still a way to go for her feelings to catch up.

She followed Samuel to the car, running her hand through Bruce's soft, dense fur as he pushed past to jump into the back seat. She slid into the front.

Samuel climbed into the driver's seat and reached into the console. He handed her a new cell phone. "Thought you might need this."

"Thanks. What do I owe you?"

"Consider it a gift from the Cordova PD."

Rachel's heart warmed. Most likely it'd been paid for from Samuel's own wallet, but that was okay. He cared.

They drove home, and a light misting of sleet

triggered the windshield wipers. Eyak Lake disappeared, enveloped by hovering clouds.

"Blizzard conditions are forecasted sometime over the weekend." The grim tone of Samuel's voice replenished the sense of foreboding in her gut. "You have enough supplies to last if you get snowed in?"

Rachel nodded. "I think so."

"Let's check when you get home."

They pulled into the driveway, and Samuel held his jacket over her while they raced through the sleet to the front door. Bruce snapped at the sleet and barked with excitement.

Samuel went back for the bags, and Rachel took off her wet coat. Rather than easing up, the sleet drummed at the windows like a stampede of caribou. She rubbed Bruce down with a towel before Samuel returned, stamping his feet before coming in.

"Won't the roads be slippery now? I'm worried about Katie."

He parked the bags to the side before removing his own coat and hanging it on a hook. "Everyone's trained to drive in these conditions. Officer O'Halloran's no exception. She'll get home safely. Can I make you some coffee?"

Rachel sighed, recalling the coffee and eggs he'd made only days ago. The fantasy of Samuel being here as more than a guest felt nice, but unrealistic. "I'll do it. You sit."

Samuel didn't argue, instead he went to the fireplace and laid the fire. So much for him being the guest. It caught by the time the coffee had brewed, and Rachel found half a pack of chocolate chip cookies to go with it.

"Thanks, Samuel." She brought a tray loaded with the coffee and cookies over to the fireplace.

He accepted a cup and a cookie. "Never met a cookie I didn't like."

She chuckled, then sat on the chair near the fireplace, sipping her coffee. The smells of woodsmoke and arabica beans mingled pleasantly.

"Do you mind if I ask you a few questions about Donal Hayne?"

Rachel stiffened at the name, then forced herself to relax. "Sure. Did you interview him?"

"Yeah, but you know I can't tell you anything, right?"

"Can you at least say if he told you why he did it?"

Samuel drew a deep breath. "All I can say is we might know more on Monday after the arraignment."

Rachel's shoulders drooped. Donal Hayne had told him nothing. And a whole weekend stretched ahead of them before the possibility of knowing anything. "Okay, thanks."

"Look, we have procedures we have to follow. That's all." He ran his hand over his hair. "I know you've already said you didn't know his name and haven't recognized his photo, but we think he might've known Hank. Where might he have known him from?"

"Hank? Really?" She felt exposed. "If he knew Hank, does that mean he..." Unable to say the words aloud, she sipped her coffee.

"Any physical evidence we might've got from the car was destroyed, but given the circumstances, I believe it's still worth widening the investigation to include their deaths. Chief Anderson agrees, and he has other officers going over the evidence from each of the other crime scenes to find any similarities. I'm working this angle with O'Halloran, so anything you might remember could help. Did Hank have particular hobbies or other interests?"

Rachel's heart rate picked up. It sounded like the police were taking this seriously. "Everyone knew Hank, but I guess they mostly knew him because he was a friendly guy. Donal Hayne probably talked to him. Hank worked FIFO at Prudhoe Bay for a long time, but he didn't like leaving Katie and Sarah, so he got a job with the USDA. He'd worked there for about six months before..."

"Before he died." Samuel gave her a sympathetic look. "That's good to know. Might be a work connection. Anything else?"

Rachel shrugged. "Hank liked nature. He went

out and about in the wilderness every chance he got. Maybe they met out there." Hank's love of nature was the reason the family had purchased a house so far out of town. He and Sarah had wanted Katie to enjoy summers picking wild blueberries and fishing for sockeye. The big happy family they'd planned for their little girl would never eventuate. A weight settled in her chest. "I haven't been through Hank and Sarah's things. Should I look now?" A job she'd dreaded and put off.

Samuel reached over and squeezed her shoulder, sending a tingle down her arm. The scent of his aftershave added to the coffee and woodsmoke. "It's fine. We'll follow up the leads. If we don't find anything, we can go through their things together." He stood. "I'm going to bring in a little more firewood for you, and you check the pantry. Make sure you have everything you need."

Rachel stood with him. "Samuel?" She touched his sleeve and he turned, waiting for her to continue. "Thank you. For everything. What you're doing is above and beyond your duty." She licked her lips and gave him one of those smiles that were as rare as a view of Denali's peak, and just as beautiful. "I appreciate it."

"I'm not here just on account of duty." He took her hand, and her breath hitched as he looked into her eyes. He leaned forward until his face was inches from hers and whispered. “Rachel, I want to kiss you.”

She closed the distance, pressing her lips to his. He enfolded her in his arms just as Bruce’s barks startled them apart.

ELEVEN

Bruce's bark heralded the arrival of Officer O'Halloran and Katie, and Samuel pulled away. His eyes didn't leave hers until he turned and walked toward the front door. The intensity of her feelings terrified her. *I shouldn't lead him on when I can't imagine him in my life. Why did I kiss him?*

Katie interrupted her chain of thought, bounding toward her with a bag of shopping. "Jock brought marshmallows! And chocolate! And graham crackers!"

"Why don't you go show Officer O'Halloran where they go?" Rachel's heart raced as Katie bounded toward the kitchen followed by O'Halloran.

Samuel wasted no time taking her hand, but Katie's voice echoed from the kitchen before he spoke. "Aunt Rachel!"

He licked his lips. "I'll call you tomorrow when my shift's done. We can talk about… us."

There is no us. She couldn't say it now. Not after that kiss.

All too soon, O'Halloran, Samuel and Bruce were gone. O'Halloran had brought extra supplies with him, so Katie had been stuffed full to the brim with s'mores and hot chocolate.

"I miss Bruce and Samuel." Katie echoed her own thoughts as their absence descended. "I miss Miss Ryder, too." She giggled. "Miss Miss. That's two *misses*."

Rachel reached out to pull Katie into a hug. "I miss them, too, Kitty-cat. But you'll see Miss Ryder tomorrow if the weather isn't too bad. Now come, it's bedtime. Let's get you tucked in."

Katie ignored her. "Jock's funny. He told me about Bruce when he was a newborn puppy. Soooo cute!"

"Katie..."

"I know, I know, bedtime." She gave an exaggerated sigh.

Once Katie was safely tucked in bed, Rachel's mind returned to Samuel's kiss. The thought of his arms around her made her go all gooey inside. How she longed for things to be different. *Stop your foolish daydreaming and focus.* She stretched her arms over her head. No use putting it off any longer. She logged onto her laptop, opened a browser and did what she'd been planning to do since she'd heard the name *Donal Hayne*.

Her search returned an actor with a similar name, along with some racing results. But as she scrolled down, no one mentioned could be the man who'd attacked her. Then, on about page three of the results, she came across a photo of a tall, thin man standing with a woman holding a baby, along with two small children. They stood together on a picturesque summer's day, in front of a low fence similar to Sarah and Hank's—the one out back that separated the property from the Sitka spruce and hemlock of the forest. Must be his family, before the divorce. The younger child looked a lot like Lotte, one of Katie's friends. What was her mom's name? Rachel closed her eyes. It must be on the class list somewhere. She logged into her email and searched up the list. There she was: Mika James. Not Hayne. Maybe she hadn't changed her name when she'd married.

Rachel ran her hands through her hair. If the mom had been friends with Sarah, wouldn't she have seen her at the funeral? Wouldn't she have reached out? The connection couldn't have been that strong, but she'd still let Samuel know. She wrote down the details and printed off the photo. Her eyes drooped, and she rested her head on her hands. Maybe if she closed her eyes for a few moments…

The next thing she knew, Katie was poking her awake. "Aunt Rachel, why are you wearing the same clothes as yesterday?"

Rachel sat up with a start, rubbing her eyes. So much for closing her eyes for a few moments. The clock read eight thirty. "Good morning, Kitty-cat, I must've fallen asleep. Let's get you some breakfast."

An hour later, Rachel had settled Katie in front of the television with a full tummy and a warm blanket. The wind had died down overnight, and to Rachel's relief, the sleet relented, for now. The blizzard would build in the afternoon. She glanced toward the sitting room, where Katie was already engrossed in her fairy movie, and reached for a cookie.

She picked up her phone and walked into Hank and Sarah's study. Piles of neatly stacked paper greeted her. Samuel had said not to bother looking through it yet. But what if something vital materialized? What if Hank had some connection to his killer hidden in there?

After half an hour of leafing through the papers, nothing stood out. "This is hopeless." The movie had another twenty minutes left. Should she make lunch? Then something caught her eye. A lawyer's letter with a red *COPY* stamp on it. The subject read *Letter of Demand—Donal Hayne.*

Rachel's lips parted, and she skim-read the letter. Hank had loaned Donal money. Over ten thousand dollars! From the lawyer's letter, he'd failed to repay a cent. Her stomach contracted. Had Hank been paying for Donal Hayne's child support? If so, why? Had Donal killed Hank to clear his debt? Why on earth would he be targeting Rachel and Katie now? They had nothing to do with it. Unless there was something else. She set the letter aside for Samuel and continued to leaf through the files.

Her mind wandered to Samuel as she opened the next drawer. He'd want to question Hayne about the letter, but his hands were tied until Monday. Rachel needed to know *now*. If only she could confront Donal Hayne directly about his debt to Hank. See his reaction. Find out if that was the only thing he had against her family.

She knew where he'd be held—the only place in Cordova where prisoners were kept. After searching up the number, she wrote it on the back of an envelope. She'd prefer to go in person, but no one would let her in to see a prisoner. Why not call and ask to talk to him? Pretend to be his lawyer—Samuel had referred to Donal's lawyer as *she*. She blinked rapidly. No, that would be a lie. She could just call anyway and try to convince them.

Unable to stand it any longer, she dialed.

"Cordova Police Department."

Rachel's blood curdled when she recognized Samuel's voice. What had happened to the dispatcher?

"Hello?" Samuel's voice held a mixture of concern and professionalism, not unlike the first time she'd heard it.

Rachel swallowed, then hung up. She closed her eyes. *What was I thinking?*

Her phone rang: the police number. Naturally, they knew the numbers calling in. She hadn't bothered to block it. Samuel didn't recognize the new number as hers yet. But he would. She had to answer. *What will I say? How will I explain?*

She swallowed. Time to put on her big-girl pants. "Hello?"

"Rachel?" Samuel's disbelief became obvious.

She closed her eyes, cringing. "Mm-hmm?"

"It's Samuel. Did you just call the monitored police line?"

"Yes." She swallowed. "I was hoping to talk to Donal Hayne."

Samuel exhaled. "Rachel…" He sighed. "You know that's not possible." Disappointment threaded his voice. *He probably thought I'd be calling to talk to him.* A surge of guilt rose, but she pushed it back. Her sister had to be her priority. For Katie.

"If I could just *talk* to him. Maybe he'd open up to me?" Her breath hitched. "I found something, Samuel. A debt Donal owed to Hank."

"You did?" She could almost hear the gears in Samuel's head turning. "How did you find that?"

"It was in a lawyer's letter in Hank's study. Don't worry, I've set it aside for you to look at. Please, I'd really like to talk to Donal Hayne myself."

A moment passed before Samuel replied. "You know that's not possible. You're the victim and a witness. Look, my shift finishes at noon, I meant what I said last night about calling you. Katie mentioned she hadn't had pizza in a while. Why don't I take you out for pizza and we can talk?"

Rachel sighed, then swallowed. "That'd be great."

An hour later, Katie's delight in going for pizza offset the feeling of foreboding that simply wouldn't leave Rachel's gut. Katie sat in the back of Samuel's patrol vehicle with her hand on Bruce, whose tail thumped against the seat.

"May I have pepperoni?"

"Sure, Kitty-cat. You can have whatever you like."

Her mouth dropped open. "Even a soda?"

Rachel shrugged. "A small one, sure."

"Yay!"

Samuel's mood wasn't quite as buoyant as usual. Was it something she'd said?

They pulled out of the driveway, and the fog shrouding Eyak Lake served as an ominous reminder of their first meeting. The tenuous trust that they'd built since then. Rachel's heart filled with relief when they left the lake behind and drove into town.

"We'll park outside the station and leave Bruce there. The pizza shop owner is allergic to dogs."

Rachel's stomach tightened. If the dispatcher

wasn't there, who would be on duty looking after Donal Hayne? Could this be her chance to confront him? Even if Samuel thought it was a bad idea, maybe she could convince the duty officer. "Who will look after Bruce?"

"Don't worry about him. He'll be fine in his bed."

They pulled up outside the station and piled out of the vehicle. A cold breeze swept along the street, and gulls wheeled overhead. Rachel pulled Katie's hat down over her ears, and the little girl scrunched her nose. A truck with the local café's logo pulled up beside them.

"I might use the bathroom, if I can?"

"Sure, take your time. You need to go too?" He asked Katie.

"I'm fine."

Rachel forced a smile and strode down the hall toward the bathroom and the holding cells. The officer covering the desk had his back turned on a call. Only one cell occupied. A few steps and she could peer into the cell. Ask Hayne whether he killed her sister because of a ten-thousand-dollar debt. Maybe get an answer before the officer told her to leave. Heat tingled in her face. *Samuel works here.* Samuel who had saved her life on several occasions, putting her first at every turn. He'd let her into the station today. Let her wander unsupervised because he trusted her. Because he'd *kissed* her. Any consequences would come back to him, too. *What am I doing?*

She turned and walked back to the bathroom, and a man carrying some packaged meals stopped to let her by. Surely there'd be another way she could talk to Donal Hayne. She had to think harder.

Half an hour later, Samuel chewed on a slice of pizza, his mind racing. He had less than two days to come up with enough evidence to make the case against Hayne a slam dunk. Last thing they needed would be the judge to toss the case for lack of evidence. A real possibility with a skilled lawyer and no confession. His chest tightened with the feeling he'd missed something obvious. Rachel had mentioned something about a debt. He'd ask her more when he got back to the station, but now wasn't the time. Should he even be spending valuable time eating pizza with the victim? He took another slice and forced himself to enjoy it—he was off duty, and he needed to get out of his own head. Besides, the line between victim and whatever feelings he had for Rachel had been well and truly blurred. Taking Bruce on a foot patrol around the marina hadn't helped, and neither had staring at his computer screen.

Rachel gazed out the window, deep in thought. She'd been a little off since he picked her up. Understandable, after all that had happened. She'd shut down any discussion about their relationship, using Katie's presence as a barrier. Did she regret their kiss?

"What's that?" Katie pointed to a large picture that looked like the brown-and-white spray of a wave.

The question snapped Rachel out of her daze. "I don't know, let's ask our server when she comes back."

Katie climbed down from the table and walked toward their server.

"Katie, wait." Rachel rose, but Samuel stopped her.

"Let her ask. She won't mind."

Katie reached out and placed her hand on the server's arm.

"Hello there, how can I help?" The server turned. Her bleached hair was pulled back in a ponytail, and large gold hoops dangled from her earlobes.

"What's the picture? Aunt Rachel doesn't know. She said you would." Katie's matter-of-fact manner amused the server, who walked back to the table with Katie.

"This one?" The server pointed to the photo.

Katie nodded.

"It was taken by the owner of this place at Childs Glacier. Do you know about that?"

"No." Katie's eyes grew wide.

"Well, it's about fifty miles away, near Million Dollar Bridge. You used to be able to camp there, but not too close." The server paused dramatically. "Because if you camp too close, you'll end up getting washed away!"

Katie leaned forward in gleeful surprise. "What?"

"Yeah. The glacier calves—you know what calving is?"

Katie's face wore the triumphant look of an expert. "Miss Ryder showed us. It's when a chunk of ice falls off the glacier into the water."

"Wow, you know a lot."

Glowing in the praise, Katie nodded. "I do."

"So, the glacier calves, and the chunk of ice splashes into the water and makes a big wave. Like if you drop some ice into your soda."

"Cool!" Katie dunked her hand into her soda and grabbed some ice.

Samuel stifled a chuckle at Rachel's expression when dribbles of sticky soda flowed from Katie's hand and onto the table.

"Oh, Katie, we shouldn't do that."

"It's fine, I'll clean it up. So, drop it back in." The server waited for Katie to drop it. The ice plonked back in, causing a ripple and a splash. "Imagine that but with a large piece of ice and a ten-foot wave." She pointed to the picture.

"Ohhhhh." Katie went to pick the ice up again, but Rachel placed her hand on Katie's.

"I think that's enough, Katie."

The server smiled.

"Can we go see it?" Katie asked. "Will we get washed away?"

"Well, you're unlikely to get washed away, but there's always a chance. The largest wave I know about was thirty feet, and that happened in 1993. But it usually reaches ten feet every other year and five feet a couple of times a year." She took out a cloth and wiped Katie's mess away. "You can't get there at the moment anyway unless you have a boat. Bridge 339 washed out before you were even born."

"Awwww, I want to see it."

Rachel smiled her thanks to the server. "Maybe one day if the bridge gets fixed. How about you finish your pizza?"

"Okay, fine."

"I should get back to Bruce," Samuel said. The tenseness in his muscles said more about his reluctance to leave Rachel and Katie than anything else. Could he invite himself to dinner tonight? No, he had a day and a half to get this case sorted out, and Rachel didn't seem to be in the mood for company.

They walked back to the station, Katie skipping along the edge of the sidewalk, avoiding the cracks. Samuel resisted the urge to take Rachel's hand in his. The blurred line of their relationship couldn't handle it.

An ambulance—back doors open—was parked

out front of the station. Samuel quickened his pace. Someone was being treated in the ambulance, and O'Halloran stood outside, hands on his hips.

Samuel held out his arm to stop Rachel and Katie advancing. "Why don't you go wait with Bruce?"

Rachel's brow creased, then the word "Clear!" from the paramedics startled her into action, and she took Katie with her.

Samuel rushed toward the ambulance. "What's happened, O'Halloran?"

"I don't know. The prisoner just collapsed in his cell. He didn't respond, so I called the paramedics. They got him out here, and now…" His voice trailed off when one of the paramedics stepped out from the van shaking his head.

"Sorry, fellas, we couldn't save him."

Samuel's gut curdled. There was only one prisoner: Donal Hayne. "What happened?"

The paramedic shrugged. "Cardiac arrest. The coroner will have to find out what caused it."

The other paramedic stepped out from the back, removing his latex gloves. "His blood looked cherry red when we ran the IV. Could be cyanide poisoning. The autopsy will tell you for sure."

Samuel swung around to O'Halloran. "What did he eat?"

O'Halloran shrugged. "The usual catering. I

think it was soup today. I'll go bag whatever's left."

"Can you sign this, please?" The paramedic held out a clipboard to Samuel.

Samuel signed the form, then waited for the paramedics to pack up and leave. It couldn't be poisoning, surely. The only person with a motive was Rachel. *The bathroom is right near the jail.* No, she wanted answers. Wouldn't get them with a dead prisoner. Someone wanted him dead, though, and bad enough to risk doing it in the police station.

His mind flicked to the lawyer. Could someone else be in the mix? Someone who didn't want Donal Hayne to talk? But why? What did that have to do with Rachel?

Rachel. The hair on the back of his neck stiffened. She'd be inside, wondering what had happened. The ambulance pulled away, and he headed into the station.

Katie and Bruce lay next to each other on the floor, playing some game that involved Katie high fiving Bruce while his tail wagged with boundless enthusiasm. Rachel sat on Samuel's desk chair, kneading her hands in her lap.

"Bruce." Samuel's command got his attention. Katie rolled up to sit with a giggle. "Sorry, Katie, when Bruce is in the police station, he's working."

The husky tossed his head, then came to heel.

Katie stage-whispered, "I'm going to get you treats from Jock."

Rachel stood, smoothing her pants. Her eyes followed Katie, reassured when O'Halloran acknowledged her. Her gaze met Samuel's. Why were her cheeks flushed?

Sweat beaded on her brow. "Is everything okay? Jock didn't say anything."

Samuel pursed his lips. Was it good news or bad news? On the one hand, Donal Hayne could never hurt her again. On the other, if there were more to this, their one lead to get to the truth was gone. He swallowed. "Donal Hayne is dead."

Rachel gasped. "What? How?"

No way he'd tell her the paramedic's suspicions. He shrugged.

"I can't believe it! I didn't even get to talk to him. I should've just—" Her hands covered her mouth, and she darted a glance at him before averting her eyes. Why did she look so guilty?

Had she slipped in and convinced the duty officer to let her see Hayne? Doubtful. He didn't want to treat Rachel with suspicion, but he couldn't let his feelings cloud his judgment. This needed careful treatment. Samuel didn't like asking questions to which he didn't know the answer. But Rachel's emotions were an open book. Her reaction would tell him what he needed to know. He crossed his arms.

"Did you see anything suspicious before we went out for pizza?"

Rachel's cheeks flushed. "Um, just the caterer. He pushed past me with a box when I came out of the bathroom." The red of her cheeks deepened.

The explanation seemed plausible, but she was hiding something. What? He'd focus on the caterer for now; that might lead her to the whole truth.

"Why did you think he or she was a caterer? Did they have a uniform?"

"Yes, though I didn't recognize his face. He wore the café uniform, but he isn't a regular worker, I don't think. I mean, I've never seen him."

Samuel's ears pricked. O'Halloran had said the catering was the usual. If Hayne had been poisoned, he'd have to interview the café staff. Maybe one of them had a connection to Rachel.

"Did you notice anything else unusual about him?"

Rachel sucked in a deep breath. "I want to be honest with you, Samuel, but if I am, you'll think less of me."

Samuel's stomach hardened. He was about to get what he wanted, so why did it make him feel so bad?

"I had planned to try to see him. Donal Hayne, I mean, even though you said I couldn't." She risked a glance, and based on the recoil in her eyes, he must be glaring at her. He tried to soften his face.

"Did the duty officer turn you back?"

Rachel swallowed. "No, it didn't get that far. I didn't want you to get into trouble. You let me into the station. If something had happened..."

"Something *did* happen." The words came out colder than he'd meant. He couldn't begrudge Rachel wanting to know more, and she'd done no real harm. The fact she'd owned up and hadn't tried to hide her deception counted for a lot.

Tears filled her eyes. "I'm sorry. I didn't mean for anything to happen, I just thought if I could look him in the eye and ask him about Hank, he might tell me." She swallowed. "Do you think the caterer had something to do with his death?"

"I don't know." He ran his hands through his hair. "We don't have much to go on."

Rachel's eyes widened. "I forgot to give you this." She rummaged in her handbag and pulled out an envelope. "It's the legal letter I told you about. The money Donal Hayne owed to Hank."

Samuel pulled the letter from the envelope and read it. The name of the lawyer caught his eye: *Harriet Callinan*. Donal Hayne's defense attorney. Acting for Hayne and Hank would be a conflict of interest. There must be more to this.

Did the lawyer pay off the caterer to poison Hayne? Was she worried that Hayne would confess and drag her into it? Could a third party be involved?

Samuel shook his head. All he knew for sure was that Hayne had tried to kill Rachel and might have killed Hank and Sarah. If someone had killed *Hayne*, then it was probable Hayne had been working for someone. And that person probably wanted Rachel dead.

Rachel remained in danger.

TWELVE

Rachel's heart raced like it might explode. Donal Hayne, dead? How was that possible? Now they'd never know what had happened. They'd never know for sure whether he killed Hank and Sarah, or why. And Samuel seemed to think there could be foul play. What did that mean for her and Katie?

"Who would like a sleepover with Miss Ryder?" Samuel locked eyes with Rachel, a silent warning not to question him.

She forced out the reply. "We'll have to go home and get some things." Was this a precaution, or was there something he hadn't told her? She plodded toward the front of the station, following Samuel and Katie. Bruce stayed close by, nuzzling her hand as if sensing something wasn't right. She absently stroked his chin in return.

O'Halloran handed a large package to Samuel, who tucked it under his arm. "Thanks."

They reached Samuel's car, and he opened the door for Rachel, then clipped Katie in. *Donal*

Hayne's dead. The thought reverberated in her mind like an echo across the lake. Shouldn't she be happy? The man had gotten what he deserved, hadn't he? The uncertainty overwhelmed her, and she stared out the window, not noticing much except the lengthening shadows that sank into the fog.

"Rachel?"

"Huh?"

"We're here, Aunt Rachel." They'd parked out front of Beth Ryder's house, and Katie had already unclipped herself.

"Don't we need to get our things? Will Beth be okay with this?" Her futile words followed Samuel out of the car. He opened the back door to help Katie and Bruce.

Rachel shook her head and climbed from the car. Katie ran ahead to ring the doorbell.

Samuel hung back from Bruce and Katie, placing his hand on her arm. "It's better Katie stays with Beth and Bruce while we look through Hank and Sarah's things some more. I'd rather keep her out of the way until we know what or who we're dealing with. Okay?"

"Yes, of course." *What or who we're dealing with?* Rachel's stomach tormented her, the pizza now a somber weight in her gut.

Beth opened the door, and her face morphed from confusion to pleasure when Katie wrapped her arms around her. "Hi Katie, what a nice surprise. Have you come to visit?" She peered over Katie's head and shot a questioning look at Samuel.

"Do you mind if we come in?" Samuel gestured for Rachel to go before him. "That wind's picking up, don't let it chill your house."

"I just put a batch of blueberry muffins in the oven, maybe you and the teddy bears can help me eat them when they come out?"

Katie's eyes widened. "Another teddy bear's picnic? Yes, please!"

"How about you come in and I'll have a quick chat with Officer Miller and your aunt."

Bruce gave Katie a gentle push in front of him, and she giggled. "Bruce wants muffins too! Come on, boy!" She rushed past Beth and scampered toward the kitchen, closely followed by the excited husky.

"What's happened?" Beth's brow creased with a mixture of confusion and concern. "I thought you had the man in jail."

"He's unfortunately passed away, but we need to find out if it was an accident or if someone else might have been involved."

Beth clamped her hand over her mouth, then pulled it away, rubbing her hands on her apron. "Katie's not in danger, is she?" She looked Rachel up and down and swallowed.

Rachel's heart fell. Beth probably wouldn't be

willing for her to stay here with Katie, and who could blame her?

"Katie's in no danger, I'm confident of that."

"Of course she can stay, as long as she wants."

"Thanks for helping, Beth, I really appreciate it. Rachel and I will go now and get what Katie needs." Samuel returned his hand to Rachel's arm and gave it a squeeze.

Beth nodded, a shaky laugh parting her lips. "Sounds good. When will you be back with her things?"

"Before dark."

"I'll say goodbye to Katie before we go." Rachel didn't wait for a response, taking off down the hall. *Lord, please don't let Katie sense my worry.* She found the girl sitting in front of the oven timer, watching the dial tick toward zero. Bruce sat next to her. His tail flicked gently from side to side, and his nose twitched.

"Only ten minutes—see, Aunt Rachel?" She pointed to the timer.

"Yum, you'll enjoy those. They already smell good." Rachel hugged Katie from behind and gave her a kiss on the cheek. "You have fun with Miss Ryder while I'm gone, okay?"

Katie turned with a frown. "Where are you going?"

"Just to get some things so you can have your sleepover. You don't even have pajamas!" How long before Katie questioned the unplanned sleepovers? It stung that little girl wasn't able to snuggle up safely in her own bed.

"Oh yeah." Katie grinned. "Thanks." She stood and turned to give Rachel a bear hug. "Love you!"

A lump grew in Rachel's throat. "I love you, too, Katie."

"Bruce!" Samuel called the puppy, and he raced back to his master.

Rachel sniffed back the tears that wouldn't go away. "See you soon."

"Bye!" Katie sat back down, and Rachel trudged back to the front of the house. If this was the right thing to do, why did it feel so wrong? She went to Beth and hugged her, then pulled back and looked her in the eye. "I don't have the words to tell you how grateful I am for you. Please, when this is all over, can we get together and talk? Even though I can never repay you for all you've done for us, I'd love to do *something* for you. And to get to know you better. Even something as simple as coffee and a chat. Or a donation to your favorite charity." She huffed a tearful laugh, and Beth swiped her own eyes.

"That would be lovely. I'll look forward to it. Don't worry about Katie. I have her covered."

Rachel gave the woman one more hug, then followed Samuel out of the house to climb into the car.

She stared out the window while Samuel navigated them out of town. Fog spread across the road, and their tires slipped every now and then on the ice. Did he notice her startle?

"I'm staying with you, Rachel. You're not leaving my side until we get to the bottom of this."

A tingling warmth threaded through her limbs, and she bit her lip, not trusting herself to speak. Samuel wouldn't leave her. Even after her deception.

"I don't like this weather," he said. "Think I'll put the chains on when we get to your house. Don't want to get caught out."

"We won't be staying there tonight?"

Samuel's hands tightened on the steering wheel. "Let's go one step at a time."

Her stomach quivered. She had to be okay with uncertainty. Most importantly, Katie had somewhere safe to stay. "Okay." But Rachel had one more question. "Do you still think Donal Hayne killed Sarah and Hank and tried to kill me?"

They pulled into the driveway, and Samuel parked before answering. He turned to her. "I think he tried to kill you, and it's possible he killed Sarah and Hank, but there's not enough evidence to know for sure."

Rachel's shoulders drooped. "I wish we could be certain."

Samuel pressed his lips together. "I can keep investigating."

"Do you have any idea who killed Donal Hayne?"

Samuel took her hands in his. Their warmth made her realize her own were freezing. "I don't know for sure anyone did. But if someone else is involved, we'll find them."

He handed her a box. "Here are your father's belongings. You can look through these while I check out Sarah and Hank's files."

"Thanks." Rachel's mind raced. Maybe there would be some answers in the box. She clutched it to her chest and followed Samuel toward the house. Beside him, Bruce growled. Before she could think anything more, Samuel had reached for his gun and pushed her behind him.

"Wha—" The front door stood ajar. Rachel's heart dropped. Was someone inside?

Adrenaline coursed through Samuel's veins. He hadn't expected someone to come to Rachel's house. Whoever had poisoned Hayne—and Samuel was more convinced than not the man had been poisoned—had been careful. Why would they expose themself now?

He pursed his lips. He'd prefer to take Rachel straight back to the station, but he couldn't afford to leave the house without searching it. In the unlikely event someone remained inside, he needed to get him—or her—and finish this now.

"Stay close." He patted his leg, bringing Bruce to heel.

Rachel tucked in behind him as they edged toward the front door. Her hand grasped his arm, and her breath warmed the back of his neck.

No point announcing their location, an intruder would've heard their vehicle already.

He eased the door open. Nothing.

They stepped into the entrance. Silence, except for the wind whistling through the Sitka pines. That blizzard approached fast. He locked the door behind them, then cleared the kitchen, living room, each bedroom. Bruce whined and pawed at the door to the basement, and Samuel headed toward him, opening the door. They paused on the basement stairs.

"You think he's down there?" Rachel's tremulous whisper filled his ear.

"No, Bruce would've shot down the stairs right away. But let's check. Something's bothered him."

He flicked on the light at the top of the stairs and surveyed the basement. Bruce sniffed, searching, but didn't fix on anything. Nothing out of place, except… "Did you leave the furnace on?"

"No." Rachel's grip on his arm tightened, and her breath hitched.

They crept down the stairs, and Samuel cleared the basement, then checked the furnace. Someone had been here, all right. Furniture had been moved, revealing imprints on the floor.

Samuel lowered his weapon and tucked it into

the holster at his side. "Whoever was here is gone now."

Rachel's shoulders sagged. "How did he get in? I had the locks changed after Hank and Sarah passed, and I haven't given the key to anyone."

Samuel didn't want to scare her, but it'd be relatively easy to break into her home. The locks were not deadbolts. He ignored the question.

"Let's get your things together and go through the files."

He escorted Rachel into Katie's room, and then hers. She didn't speak, focused only on the task at hand, which gave him time to think. *What did I miss?*

Donal Hayne had fit the profile perfectly. His physical description matched the perpetrator. He'd been in all the places the events had occurred without any alibi. He'd been the only person who fit all of this *and* had a connection to the family. It had seemed he'd acted alone, and he hadn't been hired—there were no unusual transactions in his account. No criminal record at all.

But how had he died? And what was the connection between his lawyer and Hank?

"I think that's everything." Rachel zipped the toiletry bag and clipped it onto Katie's pink suitcase.

"Can you show me Hank's files, please?" he asked. He released Bruce, who trotted toward the front door and settled on the mat to snooze.

Rachel led him through to a cramped room with a small desk and a bookshelf stacked with nonfiction books about birds, forestry and Alaska. A two-drawer filing cabinet held up one end of the desk, and Rachel opened it for him. "Here you go. Should I go through my father's things?"

"You can look through them in the car. I'd like to get back to the station before the weather gets worse, and I'd appreciate your help now. What have you looked through already?"

They spent some time going through Hank's files, then the rest of the study, to no avail. Seemed Rachel had already found all there was to find.

Samuel bit back his frustration. "Come out to the car and I'll put the chains on the tires."

He carried the suitcases, and Rachel trailed behind him with Bruce. He helped her into the front seat, loaded the suitcases into the back with Bruce, and retrieved the chains and gloves.

When the task had been completed, Samuel climbed into the patrol vehicle. Rachel pored over a photo album. She glanced at Samuel, her brow furrowed. "Look, isn't that Donal Hayne?"

Samuel leaned over to see. A group photo, maybe two dozen people standing in front of a drill site. Most of them wore protective clothing and hard hats. The other few looked like executives or project managers. The photo might be ten years old, but the man in the back row was unmistakable. He nodded. "That's him, all right."

"But look who else is in the photo."

Samuel followed her finger.

"It's my father! Hayne *worked* for my father's company! Not just as a pilot but as a driller. Do you think that's the connection? Some of the employees have a problem with our family? But how would they know the connection between my father and me?" She pursed her lips. "It would have to be someone who knew us all before my mother moved Sarah and me away. None of them look old enough for that."

Samuel's eyes were drawn to the man standing next to him. The man looked about the same age as Hayne. Something about him seemed familiar. "Doesn't that man resemble the woman in the photo of your father's first wife?"

Rachel took a closer look. "Yes, you're right." She scrabbled around and pulled out the photo to compare it. "Do you think he might be related to her?" She gasped and her hand leaped to her mouth. "Do you think he might be related to my father? To me?"

Samuel considered that. Could the man be the child of Rachel's father and his first wife? A half brother to Rachel? "Maybe. What else have you found?"

Rachel leafed through the papers. "I haven't had a chance to go through everything. Got caught up in the pictures. Do you want to look?" She thrust a pile of documents into his hands.

He leafed through the documents. Property titles, tax information, share certificates. Then he found a folded document with a large red-stamped *COPY* at the top. Opening it, he turned to Rachel. "Last Will and Testament of Johnathan Maynard Bishop. You should probably read this, too." He held it out to her.

Rachel let out a deep breath. "I'm not sure I want to. Will you read it?"

Samuel skimmed the legalese, getting to the guts of the document. "He's made a lawyer his executor." He raised his eyebrows. There was the connection. "Harriet Callinan. Donal Hayne's lawyer. Hank's lawyer. Finally, a solid connection." But where did Hank fit into all this? He glanced at Rachel's earnest expression. "I'm wondering if it's a motive. With your father's death, she controls the estate."

"Surely my dad put her in charge for a reason. Up until his death, he ran a billion-dollar business, so he knew what he was doing."

Samuel shrugged. "You're right. It's not unprecedented to put a lawyer down as an executor. Sometimes it's easier with complicated estates, and from the size of this will, I'm guessing it's pretty complicated. The property is dealt with in parts. He's left his home to a children's charity." *But what about the connection with Hank and*

Donal Hayne? Something niggled at the back of his mind.

"Looks like he's left his boat to the boating club. Personal effects to… Austin. Who's Austin?" Samuel paused, turning the page. The next heading dealt with his shares in the oil business. He skimmed until he got to the names. "The shares in Prudhoe Oil & Gas LLC are to be divided into three equal parts and held upon trust for each of my children: Austin Charles Bishop, Sarah Louise Lawrence and Rachel Anne Harding."

Rachel gasped. Her face paled. "Austin Charles Bishop? Do you think he's the man in the photo with my father and Hayne?" She flipped through the box, pulling out the photos. "Is this my brother?"

Samuel's jaw clenched. Why hadn't anyone mentioned a son?

Rachel continued to stare at the will. "He knew our last names. When he wrote it, my father knew I was alive! When did he write it?"

Samuel flicked to the back, still preoccupied with the half brother. "Two years ago." Was this man, Austin Bishop, still alive?

"What else does it say?" Rachel pulled the document toward her, hungry for more.

He continued to read aloud, leaning over her shoulder. "If any of my children fail to survive me by thirty days, their share shall pass to my surviving children in equal shares."

Samuel's mind turned. They had to find out if Austin was still alive. If he was, this was a real motive. If he eliminated his siblings, he'd be the sole beneficiary of the will.

THIRTEEN

A chill came over Rachel. How did she have a half brother she didn't know about? Unlike her, he'd obviously known his dad as an adult—he was in that photo with Hayne. Had Austin worked with their father?

Why wasn't he with their father when he'd died? The nurses hadn't mentioned anyone, and her father's belongings were passed to her. If Austin had been there, surely he'd have claimed his mom's rings and photos. She swallowed. Unless Austin and her father had been estranged. It was conceivable that they'd had a falling out. Her mom had left her dad, which had to have been for a good reason.

She had to admit she didn't know her father at all. He might've been a very difficult person. Maybe Austin had cut him out of his life. Assuming he was still alive. Could Austin be dead? Her mind returned to her father's will. The latest copy was dated two years ago, and her father hadn't changed his will in light of Sarah's death six months ago. Perhaps not surprising, given he'd been diagnosed with terminal cancer three months before that. He'd probably been too sick to change it. In any case, Austin had been alive at least two years ago. What else had been evident?

Katie would've been four years old then. He'd known enough to use their new names—even Sarah's married name. Must've known they were alive and even tracked them down. Had to know Katie was alive. But he didn't name her or include her in Sarah's share. Why not?

A heaviness crushed her heart. Her dad hadn't waited for her to arrive, yet he'd left her a share of his estate, to the exclusion of his grandchild. Didn't make sense. She sighed. Who did she have left in her family? Katie and maybe Austin. Although perhaps there were more. She shouldn't assume any other relatives would be included in the will when Katie hadn't been. Did she have an aunt or uncle? Cousins, even?

Samuel put the car into gear and backed down the driveway. Snow pattered against the windshield, triggering the wipers. The crunch of gravel and ice under the tires reminded Rachel of what remained at stake. Someone wanted her dead. Going through the laundry list of attempts on her life left her numb. If she died, she wanted Katie to receive her share. That would leave the little girl financially secure.

Her eyes returned to the will. Surely her father would want his granddaughter to benefit from the family fortune, too. Even if he didn't, maybe Austin would. Did Austin have a family of his own? Did he move away with a wife and a brood of children? How she longed to talk with him. Unless this was just another fantasy, and he had wanted to reach out as much as her father had.

"Do you think Austin is still alive?" she asked.

Samuel braked at the end of the driveway. "I don't know, but we have to find out. Now that Sarah's gone, the entirety of your father's oil business will go to him if you die, and he has links to Donal Hayne. It's mighty suspicious."

A low buzz filled Rachel's head. "How do we find out if he's alive? Surely he would've turned up in your searches."

"I think the best place to start is with the lawyer. If he's alive, she'll have his contact details."

Rachel's heart ached. Her whole life she'd longed to have a father. Cousins. Anyone. Now if she found she had a brother, Samuel thought he might want her dead?

Stop panicking and think.

She could talk this through with Samuel. "Okay, so we assume that Austin's alive. What do we know? He must be older, which means that he would've known me and Sarah before our parents divorced, right?"

"Yeah, makes sense."

"Then why didn't he try and find us? My friend had a third cousin reach out to her from Scotland via genealogy websites. We're siblings, isn't that even more important?"

Samuel shrugged. "Sure. Did you submit your DNA to one of those sites?"

"No, but it isn't hard to track people down these days. I have email. He's old enough to remember we existed. He could've looked us up easily enough." Her stomach lurched, and she raised her hands to her mouth. What if he *had* looked them up? "What you said before about the will. About your suspicions. Are you saying you think Austin might have paid Donal Hayne to kill Sarah?" The words came out almost in a whisper.

Samuel gave her a sharp look. "I think that's too big of a leap. We still have no physical evidence Sarah and Hank's deaths were deliberate."

Rachel's mind lurched from one possibility to the next. *Lord, is this my family's legacy? Heartbreak, estrangement and death? Over money?* Her breath quickened.

Samuel's hand reached out and took hers, giving it a squeeze. "It's going to be okay." His words calmed her.

She took a deep breath. "You're right, I'm spiraling. We have to find Austin first. He might have a heart of gold. He might even be in danger from whoever's after me."

"Let's stick with what we know. Once we get back to the station, we can investigate further and track him down." The gentle tone of his voice was reassuring.

At least I'm not alone.

Samuel pulled into the station parking lot and the windshield wipers paused midwipe. The weather had turned. Snow powdered the streets with a blizzard on the horizon.

After their discussion about her brother, Rachel had been quiet during the trip back, pawing through the contents of the box, not finding any more revelations. Her father hadn't been good at labeling photos—not that it mattered. Samuel was convinced Austin, if alive, was their best lead. There were usually three motivations for a planned murder in his experience: greed, revenge or jealousy. Inheriting a billion-dollar oil business matched the greed motive perfectly. But the theory was moot until they found out if Austin was alive. For all he knew, the lawyer could be behind the whole thing, and might have knocked Austin off, too.

His mind flicked to Harriet Callinan. Why would Rachel's father put her in charge of his estate? Rachel was correct that John Bishop couldn't be a fool. He had run that business, grown it tenfold since he took over from his own father. A shrewd businessman wouldn't be easily manipulated. Would he? Perhaps the lawyer was more to him than a lawyer? Maybe they'd had an intimate relationship. Did that explain why she was so involved in this? She'd know about his children, having drafted the will herself. Had John asked her to help Hank with the debt at a reduced rate? Did she feel entitled to a share of the estate? Would she kill to get it?

Samuel needed to more evidence before he drew any conclusions. Each possibility brought more pain to Rachel, and he'd prefer to avoid that.

Unfortunately, he'd be hard pressed to exclude her from the investigation when they'd be joined at the hip for the duration. The investigation could get a lot messier before it became clear. It could become even more painful, and he couldn't protect her from that. They'd have to sit down and face the facts together. Keep things professional. How he'd achieve that…he had no idea. Had kissing her been a mistake? If only she'd talk to him.

Samuel shielded her from the snow while they walked through the station entrance. They stamped their boots and shucked their coats, then walked into the office. Bruce shook the snow off his coat and headed for O'Halloran's pocket.

O'Halloran turned from his computer, slipping a treat to Bruce. "Didn't expect to see you back here today, but since you're here…" He glanced at Rachel, then raised his eyebrows.

"It's fine, she's going to be my shadow for now."

"Garrison and I went to the café to interview the owner. They didn't send any delivery. Someone called to cancel it."

Samuel frowned. "Did the café take the name of who canceled the order?"

"It was their busy time. The kid who took the call didn't ask."

"So anyone could have cooked up a meal and delivered it?"

O'Halloran huffed. "Not exactly. They had a uniform, truck and the correct packaging. Required some planning. The baseball cap hid his face from the surveillance camera, too, and the duty officer was distracted with a call, so he didn't notice anything apart from the uniform. Must've known about our security. But we've circulated the description Rachel gave. Hopefully, someone will come back with some information soon."

"Did you check the phone records?"

"I'm waiting for the telephone company to get back to me. It's Saturday, though, so it might not be today. I'll stay on it."

"Thanks, O'Halloran."

"One more thing," O'Halloran said. "Did you get the note on your desk? Clara called yesterday. Some records came in for you. I think she planned to email them."

Samuel's pulse raced. Clara was the court

clerk. This must have meant the records about the custody hearing between Rachel's parents had come in. "I haven't checked the email."

"I can print them for you, if that'd help?"

"That'd be great, thanks."

He placed his hand on Rachel's shoulder, and she rubbed her face and eyes. Must be tired. Probably hungry, too, as it'd been a while since their pizza. The court records could wait while they found her somewhere to eat and rest. Then they could talk.

He guided her into the break room and turned on the coffee machine. He opened the fridge. "Let's see what we have."

"I'm not that hungry." Rachel leaned back against the wall. "I should check in with Beth, see how Katie's doing. We need to drop off her bag before bedtime."

"Okay, good idea."

Rachel dialed and waited. "That's strange, it stopped ringing." She tried again. "Does she have a landline?"

"Yeah, I'll try her." Samuel's gut dropped when the answering machine picked up. He hung up. They wouldn't be out in this weather. "We should go over there."

Rachel moaned. Her eyes squeezed shut. "You think something's happened?"

"I don't know, but better to be sure. Let's go."

O'Halloran appeared at the door, a file in hand. "Here's your printing. Is everything okay?"

"We're headed to Beth's place. She's not picking up either phone."

"Beth Ryder? I'll follow you there." O'Halloran raced after them.

They pulled on their coats, gloves and hats, then half slid, half crunched through the snow to the cars. The floodlights barely pierced the darkness that had closed in. Thc crisp air burned his eyes and nose, and he hefted Bruce into the back seat, the dog unable to get a grip on the icy ground.

Samuel reached over and took Rachel's hand. "I'm sure they'll be okay. O'Halloran originally trained to be a paramedic, so if there's been an injury or something, he'll be able to help."

Rachel nodded, though her body shook, and she rocked back and forth. Her voice came out barely a whisper. "What will I do if something's happened?"

They pulled up out the front of Beth's house. Nothing appeared to be amiss. O'Halloran pulled up behind them, and they fought their way through the snow to the front door. Samuel tried the door and it opened. Unusual. Beth was security conscious, especially at the moment.

Bruce whined and bounded past them.

"Bruce!" He called the dog back to his side, then turned to Rachel. "Stay between me and

O'Halloran." He took out his gun, and O'Halloran did the same. Then they entered. "Beth? Are you here?" No answer. His mouth dried.

They hustled down the passage, clearing each room before they entered the kitchen. Bruce whined, pawing restlessly.

Rachel gasped. "Beth!" The teacher lay on the floor, her hands and feet bound and her eyes closed.

O'Halloran crouched down to check her vitals. "She's alive." He set about cutting loose her feet and hands.

"Where's Katie?" Rachel clutched Samuel, her voice shrill.

At the name, Bruce whined again, this time more of a howl. Samuel's heart sank. *If she were here, he'd have found her.*

Beth stirred and murmured.

"Beth, it's Jock. Can you hear me, Beth?" O'Halloran cupped her head in his hand. "Can someone get me a pillow or a cushion or something?"

Samuel grabbed a cushion from a stool and handed it to O'Halloran, who propped it under Beth's head.

Beth opened her eyes. "Katie?"

"What's happened, Beth? Where's Katie?" Rachel crouched down next to O'Halloran and placed her hand on Beth's.

Beth blinked and let out a shuddering breath. "He took her."

A low moan came from Rachel. "No."

"Who took her?" Samuel leaned forward.

Trying to sit up, Beth collapsed back onto the cushion and groaned. "I'm so dizzy."

"She needs water." Samuel reached for a glass and filled it. "Here."

Rachel's breathing escalated, on the edge of hyperventilation. "Please, Beth. Where's Katie? What happened?"

O'Halloran gently sat Beth up a little so she could sip some water.

"I'm sorry, Rachel. He had a gun. I tried to stop him. I stood in front of Katie, but he hit me. I think he must've tranquilized me, because I felt a needle in my neck, and the next I knew, I was tied up on the floor."

"What time was this? How long have they been gone?" Samuel's adrenaline spiked.

"I don't know. Not long, I don't think. What time is it now?"

"Going on five thirty."

Beth's face scrunched in concentration. "Around five, I think. I'd put dinner on the table. I always feed Katie at five."

"How did he gain access?" Samuel remembered the security checks he'd done.

"Katie answered the back door. I had my hands

in the suds, and I wasn't quick enough to stop her. I'm so sorry."

Rachel sobbed, and Samuel rested a hand on her shoulder to comfort her. "Not your fault, Beth. Did you see his face?"

"He said his name was Austin Bishop. Made me repeat it so I wouldn't forget. He said to make sure you knew he had Katie."

"No, oh, no." Rachel broke down, her shoulders quaking.

That answered their question whether the man was alive. "Did he say where he was taking Katie?"

"No."

Rachel's voice cracked. "Where would he go?" Fresh sobs wracked her body, and she gazed up at Samuel.

A lump rose in Samuel's throat. He had no idea.

FOURTEEN

Rachel hadn't experienced such intense pain before. Not when Sarah died. Not when her mom died. Not even her father. A vise squeezed her heart like it wanted to stop its beating. What did Austin want with Katie? Samuel crouched in front of her while O'Halloran attended to Beth. He searched her face.

"Why Katie?" The little girl would be so scared. Unless he'd tranquilized her like he'd done Beth. The thought made her shudder. Katie hated needles.

Samuel took her hands in his. "We need to think where he'd take her. Do you have any ideas at all?"

Rachel racked her brain. She knew as much about Austin as Samuel did. Looking through her father's belongings didn't tell her much, except he'd been at the oil fields with Donal Hayne and their father. "He wouldn't take her to the oil fields, would he?"

"No way he'll make it far in this weather. He'll have to lay low somewhere until it's over."

Rachel's eyes widened. Maybe Austin had been the intruder at her house earlier. "The only place that makes sense is Hank and Sarah's."

"Okay, let's go." Samuel started for the front door.

"What about Beth?" The responsibility of involving Katie's teacher in this situation weighed heavily.

"O'Halloran will stay with her. She'll be okay." He squeezed her hands. "You're right, Austin is probably the one who broke in and turned on the furnace. Who knows why, but there's been no other clue." He hesitated, like he'd wanted to say something more but thought better of it.

The snow continued during the drive. Rachel was grateful Samuel drove as the blizzard closed in. A Land Rover with an empty trailer and chains had parked in the driveway. Lights shone from the windows of the house.

Rachel gasped. "They're here."

Samuel nodded and pulled the vehicle behind a stack of wood. "We must be careful. Austin is armed, and he has Katie. We don't want any shots fired if we can help it." The unease in his voice was evident. "Climb out the driver's side. It's more sheltered."

Rachel did as he said, and he helped her from the vehicle. Tiny particles of ice battered them while they crouched behind the vehicle. Bruce turned his ears and tail inward, and she pulled the hood of her coat tighter around her face and licked the tang of cold snow from her lips. *How does it taste? Cold.* A poignant reminder of Katie's routine. *Please, Lord, let me hear Katie's voice again.*

"I want to scope out the house before we try and enter. We'll go clockwise, starting at the west, okay? Stay close." He had to raise his voice over the gale, and he kept his gun holstered. Gripping her hand, he crouched and pulled her after him toward the side of the house. Bruce tucked in beside them, the warmth of his fur against Rachel's leg.

Rachel's heart pounded.

Each window had the curtains drawn, but no shadows crossed them. Maybe he had Katie in the lounge on the other side of the house.

The wind had picked up, and the blizzard buffeted them at each step. Ice skittered along their bodies, blown by the harsh wind. Rachel's face stung from the cold, and her nose ran. Frost clung to her eyelashes. She couldn't feel her fingers. The urgency she felt to get to Katie gnawed at her stomach.

After what seemed like hours, they reached the front of the house. No sign of anyone. Where were they?

Samuel braced himself against the front porch.

"This is a whiteout. Stay behind me." He tried the door. Locked.

Rachel's body shivered from cold as much as fear. She handed Samuel the key, nearly dropping it. He turned the key and stepped back. Nothing.

He spoke into her ear. "I'm going to open the door and go inside with Bruce. Hold the storm door open. If it's safe, I'll call for you to come in, okay?"

It wasn't in any way okay, but what choice did she have? "Fine." Her lungs burned from the prolonged cold, and she longed to close her eyes and sleep right there. Then hopefully wake up from this nightmare.

Samuel disappeared into the house, leaving the front door ajar. Moments later, he called out, "Come in, Rachel. They're gone."

Rachel's head spun as she rushed in through the door, slamming it behind her. How could they be gone? The Land Rover was here. Where was Katie?

Samuel went ahead, but Rachel paused at Katie's bedroom door. Everything was exactly as she'd left it. Had they come inside at all?

Bruce snuffled and huffed, and Rachel gave him a scratch on the ears. "You miss her, too, don't you, boy?"

Samuel's voice echoed down the passage. "I'll light a fire."

Rachel's heart raced. Why light a fire when

they had to find Katie? Snow pelted the windows, and the wind whistled along the walls. She opened a curtain and peered out. They couldn't go anywhere if they tried. How would Katie fare in these conditions? *Lord, please keep Katie safe. Please give Austin the knowledge to survive with her.*

She turned to sit at the kitchen table, flexing her fingers to get the feeling back into them. An unfamiliar phone lay in the middle of it.

"Samuel, is this your phone?" Her lips trembled as she spoke.

A match struck and a fizz and crackle emanated from the fireplace. "Hold on, I'll be right there."

Rachel picked up the phone. A prepaid flip top. She opened it. One preprogrammed number, ready to dial. Should she call it? *Wait for Samuel.* She stepped into the living room where Bruce sat in front of the fire next to Samuel, who blew on the small flames, adding twigs as he went. He glanced at Rachel, and she handed him the phone.

"Where did you find this?" He stood, examining the phone, his eyes narrowed with wariness.

"On the kitchen table."

Samuel sighed. "He's playing a game." He called the number. His shoulders sank, and he closed the phone. "No reception."

Rachel groaned. "How long is the blizzard meant to last?"

"I'm not sure. At least overnight."

"Where would he go in this weather?"

"Wish I could tell you."

Rachel wrapped her arms around herself. "I'm going to check the pantry. Hopefully, Austin thought to take some supplies." She walked to the pantry and opened it. Untouched. She sighed. "What's he doing? I don't understand, I really don't."

"It's going to be a long night. Why don't you take a seat with Bruce, and I'll make us some food and coffee."

Where are they? The question plagued Samuel. Rachel, too, as she repeated the question every twenty minutes. She lay on the ground, her arm draped over Bruce, staring at the flames. Morning had come, but the darkness outside wouldn't lift for another few hours. The blizzard conditions hadn't let up, but he didn't dare check how bad they were snowed in. It would only add to Rachel's anxiety.

Samuel dialed the number again, hoping the battery would last—Austin had left them no charger. Still nothing. No point suggesting sleep to Rachel, but she could at least relax.

"How about I pull the sofa over to the fire? You'll be more comfortable."

He waited for her to move, then grabbed the sofa, and heaved it closer to the hearth. He'd draped his coat over the back of the sofa, and it fell off as he moved it. When he bent to pick it up, the file O'Halloran had given him fell from the inside coat pocket. He'd almost forgotten about the court files. Maybe it would give them more information about Austin.

He took the file over to the kitchen table and laid it out.

"What are you looking at?" Rachel rubbed her hair from her face and sat next to him.

"The custody documents. Thanks to O'Halloran."

Rachel leaned to read over him. "There's a lot there."

Samuel nodded and handed her some court orders. "You read those, I'll read these." He leafed through an expert-witness report from a child psychologist and froze. He read aloud. "A is a twelve-year-old boy. He has two younger half siblings—S, who is three years old, and R, who is thirteen months old. His biological father and his wife (A's stepmother) are in the process of divorcing. A's stepmother holds concerns that A is violent toward S and R." He paused and added, "Obviously A, S and R represent Austin, Sarah and Rachel."

Rachel nodded and pinched her chin.

"The father, who is the biological father of all three children, disputes the mother's claim. I interviewed A and S separately. R is too young to be interviewed, but I observed her behavior with the other children. S and R interact in an age-appropriate manner. During the observation, however, they avoided A, who sat with his arms crossed and watched them.

"A appears to be a highly intelligent child. During our interview, I noticed he was unable to empathize with others and exhibited vindictive behaviors. I caught him in several lies, and when we discussed the lies, he admitted them but demonstrated no remorse. When I pressed him on his feelings and behavior toward S and R, he refused to answer. I recommend he is referred to a pediatrician to explore a possible diagnosis of a conduct disorder."

"What does that mean?"

Samuel took a deep breath. "Well, I think there were red flags. Do you want me to read out the custody hearing documents?"

"Okay." Rachel slid them back to him.

He cleared his throat. "It describes the family structure. How Austin is a son from your father's first marriage. His first wife died soon after Austin was born, and he remarried when Austin was five years old. Your mom is frightened of Austin. There are behavior concerns, but your father didn't take them seriously. The judge then gives his findings." He skimmed the documentation and began to read about halfway through the judgment. "Based on the psychologist's report, I find that S and R should reside full-time with their mother, MB. JB will be responsible for financially supporting MB, S and R."

"I don't understand. We were always struggling. Didn't he follow through with the financial support?"

Samuel flipped through to the back of the documents. "Here's something." He pushed the paper between them so Rachel could see.

"Marriage Separation Agreement. It's dated after the court hearing." Rachel frowned and read aloud, "The parties agree the Husband shall not pay alimony to the Wife, and the Wife waives all rights to claim future spousal or child support. The Husband shall not prevent the Wife from leaving the State of Alaska. The Husband shall not contact the Wife, or their minor children." She paused and looked at Samuel, her eyebrows squished together. "I don't understand."

"I think your mom tried to protect you from Austin. She sacrificed any financial support to keep you safe." A heaviness built within Samuel when he thought of his own parents. The sacrifices they'd made, even when he'd disappointed them. If he called his dad, would he answer?

Tears welled in her eyes. "So why did my dad put us in the will? Mom was still alive when he wrote it. Their agreement would still apply."

"You were adults by then. Maybe he thought you were old enough to take care of yourselves."

Rachel wiped the tears from her cheeks.

"Sorry, I don't know why I'm crying. I don't even know what to think about this."

Samuel covered her hand with his. It was cold and he reached for the other one to warm it. "Come here." He pulled her gently toward him and wrapped his arms around her. "I'm sorry this is happening, Rachel. None of it is your fault."

A few tears slipped down her cheeks, and she swatted them away. He patted her back, searching for the right thing to say, but the fatigue of his powerlessness weighed him down. Rachel didn't deserve any of this. Austin was behind the estrangement, possibly the divorce. While Rachel's father could have probably handled matters differently, who could blame him for wanting to support his son? Had he got Austin the help he needed? Circumstances would suggest he hadn't. Now Rachel, her sister, her brother-in-law and niece had suffered. The link between Donal Hayne, Hank, the lawyer and Austin was coming into view for Samuel. It all hinged on the shares in the oil business. The ones Rachel was set to inherit with her brother. Whether Austin would reveal the truth remained to be seen.

Rachel sighed and turned her head to rest on his shoulder. He reached to stroke her hair away from his chin.

"I can't believe someone related to me and Sarah could be like this."

Samuel ran his hand over her hair, his throat tightening. “It’s a lot to take in.”

“I should never have let Katie out of my sight. I don’t deserve to be Katie’s guardian.” She rested her hand on his shoulder, and his heart broke for her. Obviously, she wasn’t fishing for a compliment. She meant every word.

“That’s not true. I didn’t think Katie would be in danger. I should’ve kept her with us.”

“Katie must be so scared and so cold.” Her voice hitched and she cleared her throat. “If she comes to harm, I don’t think I’ll ever be able to forgive myself.”

Samuel wrapped his arms around her and held her against his chest. “You did nothing wrong, okay? Until we know more, we can’t jump to conclusions. That won’t help anyone, least of all Katie.” Without thinking, he kissed the top of her head. She turned her face toward him, her red-rimmed eyes wide, lips parted.

Samuel’s phone buzzed, startling them. He swallowed. “Must have reception again.”

Rachel gasped. “We have to call.”

He dialed, switching it to speakerphone. Rachel’s breath hitched when Austin answered.

“You took your time.” Austin’s voice came out as a sneer.

Rachel spoke first before Samuel could stop her. “Where’s Katie?”

Austin snorted. “The first time you hear your

long-lost brother's voice, and that's what you say?"

Her face crumpled, and Samuel squeezed her hand.

"This is Officer Samuel Miller." Samuel kept his voice as neutral as possible.

"*Officer*, huh?"

"Is the child with you?"

Austin huffed. "She sure is, but whether you see her again is up to Rachel."

"What do you mean?" Rachel's voice filled with horror.

"Comply with my demands, or I'll dump her off Million Dollar Bridge. It will be a long, slow drowning death. Kind of poetic to die like her mom."

Rachel gasped, and confusion filled her face.

Samuel held up his hand to stop her from talking. "What do you want?"

"I *want* to talk to my sister."

"I'm here." Rachel's breathing had become ragged.

Austin chuckled. "You sound worried, sis, just the way I like it. You're going to pay for all of my misery."

"What misery?"

"No time to explain now, but don't worry, it'll all be over soon—one way or another. Now, listen carefully. You have a choice to make." He paused. "Choice number one—and spoiler alert, this is really the only choice—sign over your inheritance. The paperwork's in the cutlery drawer. If you do that, I will give you back Katie."

"What?" Rachel's mouth gaped, and her pleading eyes met Samuel's.

Austin ignored her question. "Choice number two is to not do that. In which case, you have two hours left until I dump your niece off the bridge."

Rachel staggered away from the phone, her face pale. But a slow fury replaced her fear and her jaw tightened. She lurched back to the phone. "You listen to me, you heartless—"

Samuel's heartbeat thrashed in his ears. He ended the call, snapped the phone in two, then ground it under his foot. They had to get going.

"No!" Rachel's scream pierced the air and Bruce barked. "Why did you do that?"

"He's almost certainly put a tracker, and possibly a listening device, on the phone. Now he won't know where we are, what we're doing or when we're arriving."

"He gave us two hours! What if we don't make it? We won't be able to contact him. He'll drop Katie off the bridge!"

Samuel placed his hand on her arm. "He's not going to kill his only leverage. If he doesn't get your signature, he doesn't get his payout unless he kills you. He knows that won't happen within the next twenty-eight days. You think after the efforts he's gone to, he'll nickel and dime us over a couple of hours?"

"I don't understand, surely he'll go to jail for kidnapping Katie and assaulting Beth. What's his plan?"

Samuel frowned. "Probably a really good lawyer. He probably won't serve jail time. With a billion-dollar payday at stake, and his actions so far, he's not worried about a few crimes along the way."

Rachel swallowed. "When he has the signature, he's going to kill her anyway, isn't he? And me. Leaving Beth as the only witness to any of it." Her mouth turned down.

Samuel gripped her hands in his. "He'll try. But I won't let him. I promise. Now, go get the document from the kitchen. Sign it, and I'll meet you at the front door." He whistled for Bruce, and the puppy pattered toward him with a yawn and a tail wag.

Rachel grabbed the document from the kitchen, signed it without hesitation and shoved it into her jacket. She didn't care about the money. Katie was all that mattered. She rushed to the front door and adjusted her hat and gloves while Samuel opened the door to check their way out. The snow reached three-quarters of the way up, and the blizzard continued to howl, spattering ice against the top of the glass full view storm door.

We're trapped!

FIFTEEN

Samuel's heart raced. There had to be another way out. "Let's try the back door." They ran to the back door, where the situation looked even worse. "We'll have to smash a window." He drew back a curtain. His heart sank when a snow drift greeted him. No way they'd be able to dig through that in the time they had left. He'd sounded confident when he told Rachel time didn't matter, but in reality he assumed when Austin had given them a two-hour deadline, he meant it. He raced around the house, throwing open curtains. The lack of windows that had seemed a blessing during the shooting was now a problem.

Katie's room had the smallest snowbank. Rachel had stowed Katie's pillows, blankets, and toys in the car ready to take to Beth's house, so the bed had been stripped bare. Samuel picked up Katie's desk chair and went to stab through the pane of glass, then stopped. Maybe Rachel could squeeze through. But what then? Sink into the snow?

He replaced the chair, waves of frustration rippling through him. "I don't think we'll make it through that drift in time."

Rachel shook her head. "I won't give up. Can I at least try and dig our way out the front? There's a shovel in the fireplace." Samuel nodded. "Okay. Bruce is a capable digger, too." He whistled. "Come on, boy."

Rachel grabbed the shovel from the fireplace and raced to the front door, Bruce puffing at their heels. She opened the storm door and freezing air whooshed toward them. He wanted to tell her to stay warm and stopped himself. At least digging would give her something to do. Better than sitting around worrying.

By the time he'd searched the house for supplies, and tools, Rachel and Bruce had made some headway, maybe six feet, but not enough to escape. This would take forever. He grabbed the shovel he'd found in the mud room and dug into the snow, dislodging a chunk of ice. Fifteen minutes had passed. How long would it take to get to Katie? At least an hour.

Wind howled overhead, and a heavy gust hit the roof. The snowdrift shuddered. What was happening? Was it… "Rachel—"

Snow from the roof dumped down, spilling back where they'd cleared, covering them. It took all Samuel's strength not to crumple to the ground. His arms braced against the snowdrift while it collapsed.

Everything fell silent except for his own breathing, which came in fits and starts. Was Rachel okay? He tried to move, but his back was compressed by the snow.

"Rachel? Can you move?" His voice sounded muffled, the snowdrift absorbing the sound.

He couldn't see her, or sense her, and he couldn't move. How had the snow compacted around him?

Samuel hadn't been caught in an avalanche before, but he imagined this was what it felt like. *Bruce!* Would the puppy be okay? Could he dig himself out?

The snow didn't give much when he tried to push it away, and fear threaded through him. If he couldn't move, could Rachel? Would they freeze to death while Katie drowned?

I can't do this alone. He was alone, though. Who could help him now?

Words from long ago came to him. *All that the Father gives me will come to me, and whoever comes to me I will never drive away.* Where had that come from?

He remembered. Words his pastor had spoken during a sermon so many years ago. He recalled Amanda sitting by his side. What else had the pastor said? The sermon came back to him. The Pilgrim's Progress. The man in the cage who'd resigned himself to a fiery demise. Is that what Samuel had done? He remembered the moral of the sermon. *Never. I will never drive away.* Did God accept Samuel, even after he had rejected Him? In Prince William Sound, he'd promised to do better, yet he hadn't given God a second thought since. Could God forgive that?

After all Samuel had done, all he had refused to forgive of himself and others? Would God welcome him back? *Whoever comes to me.* If today were his last, he wouldn't let the enemy take him.

He spoke into the small cavity in front of his face. "Lord, I surrender. If I die today, I will do it knowing that this is Your will. But please let Rachel survive. She's a kind person. She deserves to live a good, long life." He swallowed. "And I promise I'll go to church. Amen." He sighed. "And I know You'll love me even if I don't. Thanks for that."

Samuel turned his head when the rasping scrape of metal against snow filtered toward him. *Rachel?* Was she digging them out? Must have a greater range of movement than he did. After what seemed like hours, her boot scrabbled against his. He wriggled his body, hoping to loosen the snow. He'd lost track of her. "Rachel?" Where'd she go? What's taking so long? His scalp prickled with unease. Soon, the snow above his head opened up, and snowflakes pattered onto his face. Rachel's hand reached down to shield him.

"Are you okay? Please tell me you're okay." She spoke in fits and starts, catching her breath.

Relief washed through him, and Samuel couldn't help but smile. They were alive. "You have no idea how happy I am to see you. How did you dig me out?"

Her brow crinkled, and her breath came out in puffs of vapor. "I got trapped in an air pocket. The compacted snow from the blizzard shielded me from the worst of it. But I can't find Bruce. Do you think he made it back into the house?"

"I don't know." Samuel twisted and squirmed until his arms were free. He hauled himself into the space Rachel had left.

Suddenly, Bruce's paws scraped along his thigh. Samuel laughed. "Good boy! Good dog!" The husky sure knew how to survive. He waited for Bruce to keep digging. Snow fell away around him—must've left some air pockets. *Thank You, Lord!*

He hauled Bruce into the air pocket. Bruce woofed and licked Samuel's cheek. "Okay, boy, I love you, too." He gave Bruce a hug and ruffled his fur. "Good dog!" He boosted Bruce up to Rachel, who held him steady. "How did you get up there? I can't find any footholds."

"You're on the stoop. Just kick around until you find the rail."

Samuel found it, climbing up to join Rachel on the roof. He pulled her into his arms and held her tight. The blizzard had eased now, and small flakes of snow were all that remained. He looked around them. His gaze paused on Hank's shed. The doors hinged inward as well as outward.

"I need to pray." He bowed his head. "Lord, thank You for hearing my prayers. Thank You for keeping Rachel safe. Please help us now to find Katie and keep her safe. Amen."

"Amen." Rachel's voice caught and she turned to face him. "That's the first time you've prayed."

"The Lord found me in the snow and kept His promise. I'm going to keep praying until He calls me home."

Rachel's eyes filled, and she gently bit her lip. "Really?"

Samuel nodded. "Let's trust Him to help us get Katie back." He reached over to brush some ice from hair, and something in his heart shifted. His feelings for this woman were different from those he'd had for Amanda. Rachel had a depth and an honesty that drew him to her. She wasn't tough, like the military wife Amanda had been, but she wasn't a pushover, either.

At the sound of Katie's name, Bruce whined and nudged between them. Samuel cleared his throat, wrenching his eyes off Rachel. He'd had no warning Amanda would be in danger, but he had no excuse with Rachel. He had to protect her. Them. "Let's go find Katie."

Rachel adjusted her hat. "How are we going to get to her? The roads will be impassable. Even if we can dig out your SUV."

Samuel gave her a squeeze. "Hank has a snowmobile, and I'm sure he has fuel as well."

"I didn't think of that!" She smiled, but just as quickly the smile left her face. "Million Dollar Bridge is right near Childs Glacier. Didn't that server tell us that the bridge was down? How will we get there without a boat?"

"Let's get as far as we can and pray that the Lord will provide." He stood and reached for Rachel's hand.

Rachel held tight to Samuel while Hank's snowmobile sped over the new drifts that coated the landscape. Samuel had estimated the journey could take between one and two hours—they had to make it in one or else…the consequences didn't bear thinking about. The weather had cleared, but the stillness and the scent of ozone remained.

Her muscles hurt from digging and exhaustion. She still had no idea how she'd managed to pull herself up onto the roof. Must've been adrenaline. That was gone now. She worried that if her heavy eyelids succumbed to sleep, she'd tumble from the vehicle. Bruce had no such trouble, tucked in front of Samuel, deep in slumber. How she hoped they'd reach Katie soon. Until then, there was nothing to do but cling to Samuel and mull over her feelings. Was the real reason she'd pushed Samuel away less about her capacity to get emotionally involved with someone, and more about getting hurt so soon after losing her sister? Loving people brought with it the likelihood of losing them. *Lord, haven't I suffered enough?*

Or was this change of heart the doing of the Lord? Had Samuel's faith played a part? Shouldn't she have faith that the Lord had a plan? Give all her fears to Him? *I'm not there yet, Lord.* She paused in her prayer. *But please don't stop working on me.*

Samuel's come to Jesus moment had surprised her. What had changed? Maybe one day he'd tell her. Whatever the reason, Rachel remained grateful. They needed all the help their prayers could summon.

She also felt thankful he'd made it out of the snow drift. The thought of what might have been made her shudder. But it focused her mind on Samuel. The fear of losing him was greater than the fear of dying.

The last time Rachel had felt that fear had been when she and Katie had left the road and plunged toward Eyak Lake. She'd prayed God would save Katie, like she'd prayed He'd save Samuel. How had Samuel become such a part of her life in just a few days? How did she feel like she knew him so well? He wasn't a particularly demonstrative or emotional person. But the qualities she'd first observed had remained consistent. He was strong and brave. Protective and disciplined. She relaxed against his back, feeling the reassuring solidness of him. *Lord, please keep Samuel safe. I need him to be safe. Once he and Katie are safe, You and I can work out how I feel.*

A half hour later, they pulled up at Bridge 339. Bruce leaped from the snowmobile, wide awake, sniffing and pawing the ground. With the snowmobile turned off, Rachel's ears buzzed with the sudden quiet. A sign read *NO ACCESS BEYOND THIS POINT. SEVERE BRIDGE DAMAGE. No Pedestrians—No Vehicles. Road Closed Per Alaska Statute 19.10.100.*

Rachel's shoulders slumped. "What now?"

"We check for alternatives." Samuel climbed from the snowmobile and helped Rachel down next to him. "If Austin wants you to come to Childs Glacier, he knows it'll have to be by boat. He might have left something for you."

"Even if he did, will it be safe?" Rachel's gut clenched at the kinds of surprises Austin might leave.

Samuel shrugged. "Only one way to find out." He took her hand and led her down through the packed snow to the water's edge. Ice had started to form at the edges, and the banks were slippery.

"Let's try to stay out of the water. Don't want to have to deal with hypothermia."

They searched the banks of the river. Under the bridge, a flash of bright orange caught Rachel's eye. "What's that?" She crunched over to the orange rubber that had been partially buried by the blizzard. Samuel helped her dust off the crust of ice and snow.

"He's left us a rubber dinghy. Let's hope it has a motor, I don't like our chances of rowing our way along the river." Samuel held out his hand. "Bruce, back." He glanced at her. "Just stand back a bit while I inspect this, okay? You were right to wonder whether it'll be safe."

Thankfully, there were no surprises, and the outboard motor had been attached. Samuel untethered the rope and they carried the boat toward the water. Rachel's hands were numb with cold. If only she hadn't lost her gloves back at the house. Bruce jumped in once the stern hit the water.

"We've got about ten miles ahead of us. Let's hope there's enough fuel to make it there and back."

Rachel's apprehension accelerated when they reached the open water. Samuel picked his way slowly through the glacial silt, careful to avoid hazards. She didn't interrupt his concentration, absently warming her hands in Bruce's coat. The stroking action soothed her, taking away some of the nervous fear and tension. Bruce must be cold too; he'd buried his paw pads and nose in his fur.

What might they find when they reached the campground? Her gut churned at the thought of Katie all alone with the man from the psychologist's report. What had he done to Sarah when they were young? Sarah didn't seem to recall anything—at least she hadn't mentioned anything to Rachel. Could that explain the night terrors that had awakened Sarah every now and then, disturbing Rachel's sleep too? She shuddered.

I won't let you down, Sarah. I'll find your little girl, I promise.

The snow-shrouded peaks of the Chugach Mountains rose out of the mist. An eagle screamed for its mate, swooping over the forest of spruce and hemlock evergreens that flanked the Copper River Delta. Then the glacier appeared, a stark icy blue against the brown river.

"We're almost there." Samuel's steady voice reassured her. She wasn't here alone. If anyone could get Katie back safe and sound, it was Samuel.

Rounding the bend, the campground appeared. On the shore, shotgun in hand, stood her brother. Bruce growled, and Austin cocked the shotgun and pointed it directly at them.

Her legs weakened. *How can I be related to someone like this?*

SIXTEEN

"Stay behind me." Samuel's voice cut through her shock. He held his arm out to shield her, never taking his eyes off Austin. "Bruce, heel."

The dog obeyed, staying close to Samuel.

Where's Katie? She craned her neck, straining to see the blond ringlets that would tell her Katie was nearby. The dense brush of the national park obscured the headland. Was Million Dollar Bridge over that hill? She'd briefly glanced at the map in Hank's study, noticing the topography of the area. How she hoped Austin had tucked Katie safely on the sheltered high ground, near the bridge. Her breath hitched. Never in her worst nightmares would she have considered that someone who shared the same blood could point a shotgun at her. She stepped in front of Samuel. He shouldn't be the one in danger, protecting her. None of this was his fault.

But Samuel pulled her back, blocking her from Austin. "Stay behind me. Katie needs you."

Rachel reluctantly complied.

"Don't try anything clever." Austin's voice boomed across the water. "Come in nice and slow. And leave that dog in the boat, or I'll shoot him."

Samuel whispered. "Don't leave my side, okay? He can't hurt you if you're behind me."

"What about Katie? I don't see her." Her voice wavered.

"Bruce will find her, but I don't want to release him just yet. Austin can do a lot of damage with that shotgun. Let's go one step at a time."

Samuel switched off the motor and they coasted onto the pebbled beach. "Don't get out until I tell you. Bruce, stay."

Austin stood ten feet away, a smirk on his face. "Hello, sis."

"Where's Katie?" Rachel blurted the words before she could stop them.

Her brother chuckled, then tsked. "Patience, patience."

Samuel's hand encased hers, and he pulled her out of the dinghy. The blizzard had reached the campground, and the earth and surrounding woods were covered in thick snow. Even though their boots slid and slipped over the icy pebbles on the shore, Samuel's eyes never left Austin, and he tucked her in behind him.

"You think you can protect her from me?" The sneer in Austin's voice sent a chill down Rachel's spine. "You're as stupid as our father. He thought he could protect his precious daughters, too," he scoffed. "Fool."

Samuel moved them to Austin's left, maneuvering them so Austin had to turn away from Bruce. Maybe the dog would take the hint and get out of the line of fire.

Something told Rachel to keep him talking, even though her voice shook. "What do you want, Austin?"

Austin cackled. "What do I want? I want my childhood back! I want you to feel all the pain I felt when your mother left me to deal with our father!" He mopped his brow and growled. "I want reparations, sis."

"You want my share of the inheritance? You can have it. I've signed the paperwork."

Samuel had moved them so that they were parallel to the river. He continued to move through the fresh snow, turning Austin ever so slightly away from the river.

"Good. Hand it over, and I'll send it to Ms. Callinan to check it's all in order." He pulled out a satellite phone.

Rachel's gut dropped. "Ms. Callinan?" Her voice came out in a whisper, and Samuel interjected.

"The lawyer. Donal Hayne's lawyer. Hank's lawyer. Your father's lawyer. She's linked to everyone."

"I could've signed this at her office. Why bring me here? I don't understand."

Austin's face twisted into a sneer. "Of course you don't understand. You're as dumb as you were when you were born."

Samuel's grip tightened and his jaw clenched. "That's enough. Tell us why we're here."

"Why we're here. At last, a sensible question. This." Austin swept his arm to the side before returning it to the shotgun. "This campground is a very special place. It's the last happy memory I have." He shook his head. "I wanted to make another one, just as happy. It will be your last memory, too, sis, but it won't be happy. Now, hand over the paperwork."

Rachel pressed her elbows into her sides, trying to stop from shaking. Her brother had lost his mind, and he planned to kill her. If he had the paperwork, he'd shoot her and kill Katie—if she was still alive. She had to delay him until she'd found Katie.

"My father brought me here the weekend you and your floozy of a mother left us. He told me it was a boys' camping trip. We had a wonderful time. Camping out, roasting marshmallows. The whole shebang. But when we returned home, we learned you'd gone. When I asked if you were coming back, he said *No.* I assumed you'd all died. Do you have any idea how happy I felt? You and your sister had been the attention-sucking spawn who'd stole my father from me. Now it would just be the two of us again." His face darkened. "Until it wasn't. Daddy dear embarked on a long relationship with the bottle. And violence. I don't know whether that was worse," he scoffed. "At least the bottle didn't come back from the dead to take my inheritance."

By now, Samuel had steered them so that Austin's back was to the river. Whatever plan he had, Rachel hoped it would get them to Katie. *Where is she?*

"You're going to suffer, sis. You're going to die a very painful death." When Rachel didn't react, he continued. "You don't think I can choose how much you suffer? Donal Hayne's death wouldn't have been any more painful than a severe heart attack. That was because *I* required the hired man to use cyanide."

Rachel pressed her lips together, willing herself not to react.

"*I* ensured that Sarah and Hank's deaths were relatively quick. After the initial panic, according to Hayne, they drowned in less than five minutes. Per my instructions."

"No!" Rachel couldn't stop her reaction, hating that Austin perked up at it. While she'd known in her heart of hearts their deaths were at the hand of Donal Hayne, hearing Austin confirm it remained a shock.

He smirked. "I know *Dad's* death had zero pain because—"

"You killed our father?" Rachel interrupted with a gasp. "He was dying anyway!"

"Exactly. The morphine overdose was kindness itself. He went to sleep and didn't wake up. A peaceful way to go. I'm sure he'd agree," he scoffed. "If he wasn't so obsessed with meeting you, he'd have thanked me."

Rachel's face dropped. *My father had wanted to know me after all.*

Austin continued, "You know, Dad deserved much worse. Keeping you a secret. Right up until your dumb brother-in-law pulled out a photo of sister Sarah. He'd been showing it around, boasting, and fate shined on me. I happened to be there with the riggers. Keeping up appearances. Pretending to care about them and their families. His wife was the spitting image of Dad. Incredible. That got me suspicious, so I hired a private investigator. Lo and behold, he discovered my dear sister. Still alive and well, living in Cordova. You can imagine my surprise when I learned you were alive too!"

Rachel gripped Samuel's hand, and its steadiness fortified her. "What about Katie? Where is she?"

Austin rolled his eyes. "I'll never understand the obsession with young children. She's fine. Asleep on my boat." He shrugged, gesturing over the hill. "Well, when I say *asleep*, of course I mean out cold. Hopefully, I got the dose right."

Rachel looked around. "Boat?"

Austin gasped in frustration. "You really are as dumb as I thought. It's moored on the other side of the headland by Million Dollar Bridge. I promised I'd dump her off it, didn't I? I can do that now if you want. Unless you plan to hand over that paperwork."

"Agree," Samuel whispered.

Heart racing, Rachel swallowed. "No. You're going to kill us all anyway. I'm not making it easier for you." She stepped forward, pulled the paperwork from her pocket and ripped it in two.

Samuel's blood pressure rose, and he pulled out his gun. What was she thinking? Why had she decided to risk everything when he had it under control?

Faster than he expected, Austin lunged toward Rachel and grabbed her by the hair, yanking her out of Samuel's reach. "Really, sis?" He chuckled. "You always were a little slow. That's not my only copy. I have another couple in the boat. You can sign that while I hold a gun to Katie's head. Depends on whether you're willing to risk it, doesn't it, sis? There's always a small chance I won't kill her."

Rachel's anguished cry cut through Samuel like an icy shard. He raised his pistol. Should he take the shot now? Hitting Rachel was a real risk. Still, Austin couldn't level his shotgun before Samuel could pull the trigger.

Too late. Faced with the gun, Austin smirked and pulled Rachel in front of him.

"I'm a great shot." Samuel's threat only made the man chuckle. Austin reached into his pocket pulled out a detonator. "Can you shoot me faster than you can find my boat and diffuse the bomb? It'll kill her faster than I'd hoped, but I'm flexible. Makes no difference to me how she dies. I've already planned the tragic accident. There will be no evidence." He laughed. "You have no physical evidence for anything I've orchestrated, have you? I'm home free."

Rachel gasped.

"Throw me your gun." Austin's voice lost its humor.

Samuel did as he said, and Austin threw the shotgun out of the way, reaching for Samuel's pistol. As he bent, Rachel tried to elbow Austin in the stomach, but her blow glanced off him.

Austin scoffed. "Nice try." He yanked Rachel toward the river, holding Samuel's gun to her head. "Now it's time to make sure your last moments on this earth are filled with pain."

Samuel stepped toward Austin, but the man stood his ground. "Back up!" Austin held the detonator in Samuel's face. "Yes, it's a dead man's switch. Anything happens to me and kaboom, this party starts early."

Samuel raised his hands and backed away. Where was that boat? He felt as powerless as he had at the gas station when faced with the shooter. A cold sweat broke out all over his body. *Please, Lord, I need Your help. Please answer my prayer this time.*

"Just let Katie go. You can do what you want to me." Rachel's desperation stabbed Samuel in the heart.

Austin backed toward the beach. "I'll do what I want with you soon enough. But not yet. The boat's just around the headland. We can watch the fireworks together."

Rachel's teeth clenched, and she bent her knees in an attempt to sit on the ground. Good on her, she wasn't going to make it easy for him.

Austin yanked her to her feet. "None of that, sis. You're walking every step of the way."

Behind him, Childs Glacier calved. Austin didn't notice, but the loud cracking sound caught Samuel's attention. Samuel had watched his share of glaciers calving since he'd moved to Alaska. They usually calved in the summer, but sometimes a little earthquake or a shift in the tides or the groundwater could impact glaciers year-round. The chunk of ice he'd just witnessed seemed unusually large. His mind returned to Katie's ice experiment and the words of the server. *It usually reaches ten feet every other year. The last thirty-foot wave was in 1993.* A ten-foot wave would do damage. A thirty-foot wave would wash out the entire campground.

A wave built from the base of the glacier, crawling toward the shore. Time slowed as the gigantic wave gained traction. No stopping it now. Samuel's mind blanked. Would he save them both? Or would they both perish? A sour taste entered his mouth, and the back of his throat ached when the memory of Amanda bleeding out in his arms crowded his thoughts.

Focus! He ran toward them, no hesitation this time. Didn't matter if Austin shot him. He had to get to Rachel and that detonator before the wave hit. Austin raised his gun and fired at Samuel, but Rachel struggled and strained, knocking him off balance. The bullets missed. Twenty feet and closing, but the tsunami was faster. He wouldn't make it. With a sickening, fizzy, hissing crash, the wave hit Austin and Rachel. The detonator flew from Austin's hand.

Samuel leaped toward Rachel, arms outstretched, but the wave slammed into him, throwing him backward. The water enveloped him, and a loud explosion ripped through the air. The boat! *Katie!* Samuel's heart broke in two.

Would he lose Rachel too?

SEVENTEEN

Rachel flailed in the freezing water while the swirling wave tossed her to and fro. She slammed into something hard, jarring her hip. Precious air shocked from her lungs, and she desperately reached to grab something solid. Her body was sucked into the water, bumped, and dragged across the bottom of the river.

Austin's hand remained clamped to her wrist. She tried to shake free, but he held her like a vice. *Why won't he let go?*

She remembered the bomb, and her heart thumped against her ribs. Was he gripping the detonator with the same force with which he held her wrist? If not… She struggled against Austin's hand, but his nails dug into her. *Please, Lord, save Katie.* Her heart ached for the little girl. The first time she'd held her, six years ago, she'd been brand new. A tiny, helpless, squalling bundle. Her eyes had fixed on Rachel's. She'd been entrusted to Rachel, and she'd failed. No, she hadn't. Not when she compared herself to her father. She'd been there for Katie. Maybe not as perfectly as Sarah would have, but she couldn't keep comparing herself to Sarah, or anyone else. She was Katie's aunt, and she loved her. *Lord, please help me. I need to be Katie's aunt for longer. She needs me.*

The necessity for air increased, and she started to panic. She would drown like Sarah and Hank. Her worst fear had come to pass. More than anything, she wanted Samuel. If only she'd forgotten her fears and told him that she loved him. Now he'd never know, and Katie would never have the father figure she needed. He'd revealed in his words and his actions how he felt, but she hadn't taken the chance to tell him back. What if he couldn't save her? What if he blamed himself for her death as much as Amanda's? Just when he'd opened his heart. *Lord, if it's Your will that I die today, please save Samuel. Please help him move on, to forgive himself.*

Austin's grip loosened, and Rachel's lungs burned. Was he saving himself? Or had he succumbed to a watery grave? Maybe she had a chance to survive. *Where's the sky?* She opened her eyes, but there was nothing to see, and the silt stung them. Would the last thing she saw be the glacial sediment of Copper River? It couldn't end here, surely.

Thoughts of all she'd left undone flooded her mind. Sarah and Hank's paperwork. She hadn't even buried her father. Would Austin survive to bury them both? To destroy everything Sarah and Hank had worked for? Would he become Katie's guardian? The thought sickened her. With the last of her strength, she whipped her arms and legs, trying to find the surface. Nothing. Despair made her limbs heavy, and dizziness overcame her. *Is this Your will, Lord?*

A hand grabbed her collar and pulled. Her head surfaced, and she gasped for air, coughing and spluttering while muddy water drained from her nose. Samuel's face appeared in front of her. His hands trembled, and his eyes shone.

"I thought I'd lost you."

Rachel let out a sob of relief. "Samuel! Thank God!"

Samuel shook his head, gripping her shoulders while he treaded water. "I'm so sorry, Rachel. I didn't do enough." His words seemed wooden. Why wasn't he celebrating with her? They'd survived. "Did you see Austin surface?"

"No sign of him. We have to get you back to shore. Don't want to get hypothermia." He floated on his back and wrapped his arm around her shoulder and armpit, dragging her slowly back to shore. Their waterlogged clothes weighed them down in the freezing water. The adrenaline eased, and Rachel shivered uncontrollably. No sign of Austin? They'd be able to see him if he'd resurfaced. Must've succumbed. Maybe the coast guards would find his body. *At least he can't hurt Katie anymore.*

A floating piece of hull bumped into them, and Samuel's face dropped.

"Samuel?" Rachel's brain froze, willing her thoughts to be wrong. "Why is there a piece of hull floating on the water?"

He ignored her question, grabbed the hull, and used it as a flotation device. Kicking hard, he got them back to shore. Out of the water, over the hard pebbles, onto the now-muddy bank, cold air rippled across her body. Though the snow had been washed away, the ground remained frigid. Her shivering grew worse, and her teeth began to chatter.

Samuel wrapped his arms around her in a fierce embrace. "I'm so, so sorry, Rachel." The despair in his voice broke her heart.

A deep moan arose when the thoughts couldn't be held back any longer. "Katie…"

Samuel closed his eyes, his jaw clenched. "I—" A woof interrupted him. Then another. They turned toward the campground. "Bruce!"

The puppy was dragging something. An orange life jacket. Blond curls. Red mittens. Rachel and Samuel scrambled to their feet and, with renewed strength, sprinted toward them. Bruce bounced on the spot and barked with delight.

"Katie!" Rachel collapsed next to the little girl, who was covered in sticks, leaves, and other debris, but otherwise warm and dry, and appeared to be sleeping peacefully. "She's okay!" She bundled Katie into her arms and kissed her, turning to Bruce. "You got her out of the boat? Took her to higher ground?"

Bruce's face said it all. His tail wagged, and he panted and smiled like he anticipated a large, juicy bone. Rachel planned to buy one for him the moment they got back to Cordova.

"Good boy! Good dog!" Samuel's face lit up with joy, and his eyes misted with unshed tears. He held the dog in a tight hug, nuzzling his head. "Must've pulled her out of the boat and dragged her through the woods. Even the wave didn't get her. What a good boy! You sure know how to guard!" He turned to Rachel and chuckled. "Might have some trouble getting him to guard anyone other than Katie, though."

"I'm fine with that." Rachel reached to scratch Bruce behind the ears. Her body might be freezing, but her heart was warm.

The sun beat a path through the mist, and a rainbow appeared. She swallowed, humbled by her survival. "Samuel, can we pray together?"

Bruce settled down next to Katie, and Samuel and Rachel bowed their heads in prayer.

"Lord, thank You for all of the blessings You have given us. Thank You for protecting Katie from harm. Thank You for saving us from drowning. Lord, thank You for bringing Samuel into our lives." Samuel's hand reached out for hers, and she took it. "Please watch over Katie and protect us as we return home. Amen."

Samuel continued, "Lord, thank You for giving me another chance. I pray that You will continue to strengthen my faith, and the faith of Rachel and Katie. And Lord." He paused, giving Rachel's hand a squeeze. "Lord, please bless the woman I love. Amen."

Rachel's eyes blurred with tears. She blinked them away and stared at Samuel who smiled back.

"I love you, too, Samuel. I'm glad I've survived to tell you that."

Katie's eyes flickered.

"I think she's waking up. What do we have to keep her warm?"

Samuel seemed distracted, and Rachel followed his gaze to the water. Their dinghy floated in the middle of the river.

"How are we going to get back?"

He shook his head. "Don't worry about that."

Confused, Rachel turned back to Katie, who stirred. Samuel stood and walked toward the water.

"Samuel?"

"Wait here. I'll be right back."

Rachel peered after him. Her stomach dropped when she realized where he was headed. Austin's body had washed ashore, face down and unnaturally still.

* * *

The explosion of the boat triggered an alert to the coast guard, who airlifted Rachel, Samuel, Katie and Bruce back to base. Rachel had sobbed when Austin's corpse had been zipped into a body bag. Although Katie had been given a large dose of sedative, the doctors were satisfied she'd suffer no long-term effects. Thankfully, aside from the initial shock at Beth's, she'd slept through the whole thing.

The fallout from the blizzard complicated the investigation. Harriet Callinan, the lawyer who'd played such a conflicted role within the family, had absconded from Anchorage. Officers O'Halloran and Garrison had worked overtime in the past twenty-four hours to uncover evidence of her activities, without much success. But Samuel and Rachel's statements were enough for an arrest warrant. Fortunately, the US Marshals Service had picked her up in Florida before she could board a flight to the Cayman Islands.

The laptop she'd carried with her provided evidence of her dealings with Austin. Correspondence between her and Austin included drafts of John Bishop's will and details of Sarah and Rachel's lives. She'd been working behind her client's back, feeding information to Austin in return for a substantial payout when Austin received his inheritance.

Other files contained evidence of Austin's

dealings with Donal Hayne. It turned out after he'd borrowed from Hank, Hayne had racked up eye-watering gambling debts to a gang of criminals. When Austin learned of Hayne's problem, he paid the debts to the gang on the condition that Hayne work for him off the books. Over time, Hayne couldn't kick his gambling problem. Every time he incurred more debt, Austin used him to do increasingly unsavory jobs in repayment, ending with the attempts on Rachel's life. No wonder there was no money trail—Hayne's wages had gone directly to the criminal gang. It also made sense why Hank had never been repaid.

The morning church service had ended hours ago, but Samuel, Rachel, Katie and Bruce joined Beth and O'Halloran at Beth's house. There, they read the Bible and prayed together.

"Lord, thank You for answering our prayers. You kept us safe from harm and delivered us from evil. We forgive those who have sinned against us, as You have forgiven us. Amen."

Later, once they'd tucked Katie into bed for the night with Bruce sleeping at her feet, the four adults sat around Beth's kitchen table. Beth's reaction to her ordeal had been to bake up a storm, and the table groaned under cakes, muffins, brownies and more.

Samuel guessed he'd eaten his weight in sugar, though Rachel only picked at the contents of her plate. She looked like she was about to fall asleep.

O'Halloran distracted him, his eyes twinkling. "The chief wants to see you in his office first thing tomorrow." He reached for yet another slice of lemon-drizzle cake.

Samuel grinned, reaching for Rachel's hand under the table and giving it a squeeze. "I'm sure he does."

O'Halloran shook his head with admiration. "I still can't believe you made it out alive."

"We didn't do it alone."

They nodded in agreement.

The young officer stood. "I should get back home. My shift starts in..." He looked at his watch. "Six hours."

"Thanks, O'Halloran." Samuel went to stand, but O'Halloran placed his hand on his shoulder.

"Stay there, relax. I'll see you in the morning."

Beth made up a box of cakes for O'Halloran and walked him to the door. When she returned, she yawned. "I think I'm going to turn in. Will you be okay?"

Rachel nodded. "Thanks, Beth. I can't tell you how grateful I am for, well, everything."

"You're welcome." Beth squeezed her shoulder, then walked down the hall to her bedroom.

Samuel stood, gently pulling Rachel to her feet. "Let's go to the living room. You look like you're ready to pass out." She followed him and sat next to him on the sofa in front of the oil stove. He draped his arm over the back of the sofa, trying to mask his nervousness. Then he swallowed and asked the question that had been on his mind since she'd told him she loved him. "Do you have room for me in your life?"

Rachel turned, her eyes wide. "What do you mean?"

"Your focus is on Katie. Is there room in that for…us?" He couldn't help holding his breath. *What will I do if there isn't?*

"Yes." Rachel smiled, reaching for his hand and giving it a squeeze.

Her touch flooded Samuel with relief. "I'm glad to hear you say that."

"There's plenty of room. I'm sorry I made you feel like there wasn't, and I'm sorry I shut you out. I've been a fool about all that." She turned to look him in the eye. "When you kissed me that first time, I felt guilty I'd let it happen. I didn't want to lead you on. I guess with Sarah's death and the fallout of that, I'd been so…*exhausted* thinking about the emotional energy another person in my life would take, I hadn't thought about the other side."

"The other side?" Samuel's hesitant question came out with a little more alarm than he'd meant.

She sighed, snuggling into him, her head on his shoulder. "With everything that happened, I didn't stop to realize you were already taking up plenty of emotional energy in my life. And it was effortless. Having you in my life, has been the silver lining of this ordeal. You're an amazing support. You're great with Katie. I'm sorry I didn't see it sooner." She paused, tensing slightly. "I guess my only question is about Amanda. She was your fiancée—are you ready to move on?" Her words were quiet, almost whispered.

Samuel's heart expanded. "Yes. I loved Amanda, but she was the love of Jeff's life, not mine. You've helped me to realize that the relationship I had with Amanda was more of a close friendship than anything else. She'd become my best friend, which is why losing her hurt so much. I think we'd replaced Jeff in each other's lives." He sighed. "If I'm honest with myself, I let losing her stop me from getting close to other people. I didn't want to risk losing someone I loved."

"That's understandable. I think I've been a little guilty of that too." Rachel shifted a little, turning her head to rest under his chin. "But when you're leaning on someone and then in the blink of an eye they're gone, it's hard to move on."

"I probably leaned on her a little too much." He lowered his arm until it wrapped around her shoulders. "The pain I'd caused my family… I didn't want to risk that again. Until you showed me that I wasn't the only person to suffer loss. The grace you've shown through this ordeal is humbling. You've made me realize I'm not in control, and I don't have to be. I couldn't have done anything differently with Amanda, or my family."

"Do you think you'll ever make peace with your family? I mean, you've just seen how the family feud played out for Sarah and me."

Samuel shook his head. "I'm sorry about your brother, Rachel. I know how much you wanted a family."

"I was foolish to build that idea up in my head."

"No, you deserve a good family. But, to your question about making peace…" He smiled. "I called my dad."

Rachel stirred. "You did? Did he answer?"

Samuel smiled. "Yeah. I'm taking some leave and heading back to the farm for a week or so."

"Oh." Rachel sounded disappointed, and Samuel bit back a grin.

"You know, when I left, I said that I'd be as likely to go back to the farm as I'd be to bring home a wife." He took her hands in his and leaned in until the warmth of her breath warmed his lips. "Will you come with me?"

She replied with a kiss.

EPILOGUE

Almost two years later

Sunlight streamed into the nursery, where Rachel picked up baby Sarah Valentina Miller from her crib. "Come on, munchkin, they'll be here soon." She changed the infant's diaper before blowing a raspberry on her tummy.

The fireweed had reached its pinnacle, and summer was coming to a close. Rachel looked forward to the fall colors, especially the blueberry bushes thick on the forest floor, which Katie had done a good job of stripping bare—under Bruce's watchful eye, of course. Outside work and school, the two were inseparable.

Katie skipped into the room. "Aunt Rachel, do you think Cousin Frankie will bring his own fishing rod this time?"

"I asked his mom, but it depends on their luggage. We have plenty more here after last time, though. Would you mind handing me Sarah's bunny, please?"

"Sure." Katie picked up the soft pink-flannel bunny and bypassed Rachel, snuggling it into the crook of Sarah's pudgy arm.

The front door slammed. Moments later, Samuel appeared at the door in his uniform with Bruce beside him. "How are my beautiful girls?" He kissed Rachel on the lips, then leaned down for Katie to peck him on the cheek.

Katie gave a delighted squeal. "You have prickles!"

Rachel raised her eyebrows, even as she smiled. "You're cutting it close. Don't you need to leave?"

Samuel took the baby from Rachel and gave her a kiss. Baby Sarah sighed with satisfaction. "O'Halloran's going to pick them up from the airport. We have plenty of time."

Bruce barked and raced for the front door. The doorbell rang, and Samuel's eyes widened.

"They're here!" Katie hurried after Bruce.

Rachel chuckled. "Plenty of time, huh?" She sniffed. "You might want to take a shower."

"I'll be quick."

"Come on, then. Let's go meet our family." Rachel gave Sarah a kiss on the cheek, her heart warm with the anticipation of the baby meeting her grandpa, uncles, aunts, and cousins. The big family she never dreamed she'd have.

Bruce shadowed Katie, who talked nineteen to the dozen while she showed everyone around the newly renovated and extended house. Samuel's brothers had come over to Cordova during the summer and helped him. After all, the newlyweds needed somewhere to live and raise their growing family, and Samuel's log cabin wouldn't cut it.

"Rachel!" Louisa, one of her two sisters-in-law, rushed toward her with open arms. "Your house it beautiful! The photos Samuel sent don't do it justice." She enveloped Rachel in a warm hug and kissed her on each cheek. "And the bambina, ah, what a cutie. May I?" She held out her hands to accept the baby. "Hello, little one, welcome to the family!" Louisa kissed Sarah gently on the nose, then stroked her head. "Oh, I remember these days."

Warmth radiated through Rachel's chest when the family filled the kitchen and spilled into the living room. The noise escalated, and Katie and her four cousins were shooed out into the backyard with Bruce.

Samuel's father came over to Rachel and gave her a tight embrace. "Never quiet, huh?" The wink and smile in his voice mirrored Rachel's. She, Samuel's dad and Katie were the only ones without Italian blood in the room, and it was a running joke within the family that Mr. Miller spent a lot of time out in the paddocks to escape the "rowdy Giordanos," as he affectionately called his late wife's side of the family. There was a grain of truth to the joke, though. Until Samuel had reconciled with his family, Rachel hadn't realized just how important the Italian traditions—including regular family time—were in the Miller-Giordano clan. She and Katie had embraced them, even learning how to make pasta from scratch with Samuel's nona. The old man's eyes sparkled. "How I wish Valentina was here to see this."

Tears misted Rachel's eyes as she thought of Sarah and Hank. Their house was filled with love and laughter after all. "I know what you mean."

"Now then, God always takes the bad and makes good from it." Her father-in-law gave her arm an affectionate squeeze.

An exclamation rose within the group when Samuel entered the room. Swamped by his brothers and sisters-in-law, he fought his way through to Rachel and his father.

"Pa." He embraced the old man, kissing on both cheeks. "Good to see you."

Samuel's brother, Michael, handed them each a drink. "I found the fridge."

Rachel laughed. "Glad you feel at home. I'd love a soda if you're offering."

Samuel's father walked to the kitchen to help, leaving Samuel and Rachel to watch the crowd. Sarah had already been passed from Louisa to Amalia, who cooed over the baby.

"Hopefully, this will be the first of many reconciliations." Samuel kissed Rachel on the head. "I'm so proud of you, honey."

"You took the first step, reconciling with your dad. You're my inspiration."

Sarah started to cry, and Amalia brought her back to Rachel. "This little one needs her mama."

Rachel took her back and went to the nursery to feed her.

On the wall hung the certificate of incorporation of the Sarah and Hank Lawrence Family Reconciliation Foundation. A bubble of joy rose within her whenever Rachel saw it.

Having sold her father's oil company to a local competitor, she'd decided to set up the foundation to help families reconcile. Within a year, centers had opened in Anchorage and Juneau, and when more practitioners trained, she hoped to have them throughout the lower forty-eight as well.

Satisfaction and gratitude filled her. The Lord had definitely taken something bad and built something good. The legacy of her own family's destruction now served to help other families avoid suffering the same fate.

"Thank You, God," she whispered. "For *everything*."

Samuel stuck his head in the door, his eyes soft and full of love. "Everything all right?"

She smiled. "*Everything* is just perfect."

* * * * *

Dear Reader,

Thank you for reading my debut novel. I hope you enjoyed reading Rachel and Samuel's story (and of course Katie and Bruce's!) as much as I loved writing it. These two come together at a time when their family relationships are at their nadir—a familiar experience for many, including me. When that happens, often, like Samuel, we have the opportunity to pick up the phone and offer apologies or forgiveness. Though it's not always easy! But other times, like in Rachel's position, there is no possibility of reconciliation. If that is a situation you face, I hope this story reminds you that we can always rely on Jesus, our shepherd, whose sacrificial love for each of us never fails. Even when others cast us away, He never will.

Blessings,
Megan

PS. If I can pray for you, please contact me via www.meganshort.net.